31337th Edition

RAIDING

THE WIRELESS EMPIRE

D1360602

Written by Douglas Berdeaux, and Ben Nichols

2011 – 2013, WeakNet Labs, Hax Radio, Phone Losers of America

RAIDING the Wireless Empire, *31337th Edition*

Witten by Douglas Berdeaux, and Ben Nichols
Copyright © 2011 By WeakNet Laboratories/Createspace
Printed by: Createspace in the United States
Editors: Ben Nichols, Brad Carter
Cover Design: Douglas Berdeaux

Glossary of Terms uses quotes from **Wikipedia** wikipedia.org, WPA[TM] and WPA2[TM] and word marks owned by the **Wi-Fi Alliance** wi-fi.org

9   8   7   6   5   4   3   2   1

WeakNet Laboratories: weaknetlabs.com
Hax Radio: haxradio.com
Phone Losers of America: phoneloser.org
Createspace: createspace.com

ISBN-13: 978-1456587376

Table of Contents

Conventions Used in this book:

All acronyms and technical terms are presented in the glossary at the end of this novel. All command line syntax will be in the `monospace styled font`. Thoughts by the narrator will be *italicized*. Statements held with high regard by the authors are *taller and in italics.*

Disclaimer:

This is a work of **fiction**. All names have been changed to protect the privacy of the real people <u>making it fictitious</u>. Any resemblance to actual events or locales or persons, living or dead, is entirely by common chance.

No really, If you really were hacked, **it wasn't me.** Sike.

Preface

Wireless networking completely derailed my passion for anything IT back around 2005. From the first time I went wardriving with my friends, until this day – close to a decade later, it still remains as my absolute favorite aspect of computer security. This book of **raiding** is a taste of what life is like for a **wireless** hacker within times of a worldwide computer revolution. As new technologies appear, new opportunities to hack them follow *right along*. This story starts off during the time when almost every single wireless router in the **empire** had either WEP or no security at all. To anyone new to this technology, or simply unfamiliar with anything I have written, you can check the glossary I placed at the end of the book. Thank you for reading and I will try to recall all I can from my fictitious life. Sike.

Douglas Berdeaux, 2011

Forward

In the 1970s and 1980s, it was phreaks and early hackers exploring for the fun, for the technical thrill, they were explorers in a new analogue and digital frontiers. Well, it was a new world for them at the time, for those whom lived and acted in those days. WiFi is probably the modern equivalent of some of those frontiers in terms of vulnerability, and the ubiquitous nature of its accessibility. It is this near insatiable curiosity that drives us. Let us not forget to take pause and pay homage to those who came before and paid the price for this desire. What lessons we can learn may be of significance to our present state. I offer this as a warning of self-preservation. What was once a hobby, soon became a crime, and those alchemists of old were hunted down and incarcerated. They were punished for the crime of curiosity and sentenced to live the rest of their lives as ex-convicts, outcasts or even worse, government servants. In our day and age, we walk the RF with seeming impunity, just as they did the phone lines before us. It is all too easy to get caught up in the limitless possibilities and freedom of connectivity, and so easy, it would be to ignore the silent warnings of our predecessors, that the nature of society causes those who misunderstand and fear what it is we do, which brings them to loathe us. My friends, the post-modern witch hunt is very much still underway. Do not forget, that we are both endowed and indebted by the pioneers who created this framework.

Remember to not abuse this power and access, and to protect users from those who wish to cause true harm. Let us pay homage and respect to those who came before us, and heed their warnings in earnest. For the next generation, may not hold our legacy in such regard if we do not defend these ideals.

Thanks go to John "Crunch" Draper for inspiration.

Ben Nichols, January 2011

Ch✗pter 1 - Moskau! Moskau!

In the twilight of a cold, wintery evening my life was forever changed. Although the cold was numbing, I was warm and calm sitting in the car. I was always a passenger in cars. I found a strange safe feeling in the back seat. My fear of vehicles all started from a massive auto wreck which induced a laziness that would slowly spin into a public transportation dependency and hefty traffic fines until I finally got my license when I turned 31 years old. Right now, I am 24 and sitting in my brother's car as he drives us slowly through a heavily populated apartment community in the south hills. As children we used to live in this community. It's also where I met my closest friend, Ethermine, who was sitting in the passenger side seat with his laptop open watching the screen carefully for unsecured access points.[1] Every now and then he would say "here's one" and my brother would pull the car over, switching off the headlights. We'd watch him connect to the AP, or wireless access point, and start using Google, AIM, and even check his email. It was around 2004 and we didn't know it at the time, but we were "wardriving." We were using the WiFi radio to scan for APs that had no password protection and adding the extra step of actually leeching from them. This was so enormously fascinating to me, that it completely changed my life. I wanted a laptop just for the sole purpose of doing this! I too, wanted

---

[1] Wireless access point.

to connect to other peoples APs and use their internet service to use IRC![2] I was also really poor and knew that I wouldn't have money for a laptop or credit to even finance one anytime soon...

When I think about it now, as we stray a moment into my history, I actually wanted to be a hacker since I was a teenager. I am a person who is very inspired by media. I love watching documentaries on hacking, mathematics, code breaking and science. Even though hacking scenes in Hollywood movies were always a bit corny, I admit, I wanted to hack after watching them. I started using Linux[3] when I turned twenty, introduced to me by my brother, and absolutely loved using command line tools to peek into the skirt of the internet. I started writing Bash scripts, and later I learned the programming language Perl. I *love* Perl. She is a system administrator's best friend and there is a fine line between a good system administrator, programmer, and a hacker. I started writing Perl scripts that would take user input and run the system() function to call the network command line utilities I was playing with all along. I was manipulating the output with text manipulation programs like AWK, SED, and GREP[4] and loving every second of it.

This became my second life, so to speak. My first life was dull...that is, until I started hacking and the two slowly merged together. I was working at a Subway restaurant at this time, making barely any money at all and not getting a full time schedule of hours. I *hated* it and worked late at night. Almost every shift I had, I would keep a notebook and pen to take notes while reading physics books and computer science books I scored from the local thrift shop. When helping customers, I was barely there with them or even listening at all. I would be so deep in thought that I could barely even connect to my girlfriend, family and friends most of the time. I am an obsessive

---

[2] Internet Relay Chat – an online community based chat environment that uses "channels" instead of "rooms"

[3] Linux is an operating system – like Windows or Mac OSX

[4] Generally used for splitting, substitution, and filtering (respectively) but some can do all three.

collector of information and have a very addictive personality. Usually on weekends I am too completely absorbed in what hobby or fascination I have at the moment to even consider hanging out with anyone unless it's on an IRC channel.

Sometimes on garbage nights in the city my girlfriend and I, who I lived with at the time, would drive around and pick up the old computers discarded by their owners left out by the side of the road. I used these computers to make a small network and learned about switches and routers. So, when the three of us were wardriving, I already knew a good amount about how computers and simple residential networks worked. I read a few books on upgrading and repairing PCs which taught me a lot about not only the technical aspect, but a lot of history behind the machines that I was scavenging and bringing to life. As I drifted through minimum wage jobs, I did meet a lot of fascinating, smart people. A few of them gave me books including Linux and UNIX books, modern and atomic physics books, and even their old machines when they would upgrade to new. I owe a lot to them.

After a few months of working my fingers down and showing off to my friends and family how much I was learning about computers and science, my grandmother offered to buy my first laptop, under the strict terms that I would pay her back in small increments from my small paychecks. This wasn't an easy idea to lay on my girlfriend who, at the time, thought I was wasting my time with hacking. I took the offer anyways. It was a Gateway 3040gz. She had a Broadcom based[5] 802.11 WiFi adapter, Intel graphics GPU, Intel Celeron processor, and a wide screen, glossy LCD. At the time, she was such an awesome computer. The keyboard stretched all the way from side to side. She was thin, sleek and sexy. *I called her "the Pirate Ship," and imagined her sailing the tremulous waves across the seas of*

---

[5] "based" meaning the chip-set manufacturer. Many companies make many radios, some are more compatible with pre-existing drivers to do different things than others.

RF. Pillaging and raiding, she would be feared. She would be notorious for her elite crew and arsenal.

At the time I was using WHAX! Linux And Auditor Linux on my computers and decided to go with both. I installed WHAX! Then, without formatting, ran the installer for Auditor Linux. This gave me all of the hacking tools from both distributions. Unfortunately, Broadcom drivers for Linux didn't exist and it was recommended to use NDIS-Wrapper and the actual Windows INF driver file. This meant that I couldn't play with any of the cool WiFi hacking tools that were out at the time, which sucked.

I spent a week or so researching, and I found that I could use PCMCIA adapters that had certain chip-sets in them, such as Prism, Prism2, and Atheros. My brother and I went straight to a place called COMPUSA and I bought my first D-LINK Prism2 based WiFi adapter to use with my Frankenstein Linux. When we got into the car, we decided to eat at a nearby diner and I opened the box up as we drove off. I slapped the card into the slot and ran a few PCMCIA controller commands. Eventually, I was soon up and running with Kismet! *Finally!!1/*

Later that night when I got home, after what felt like an eternity of waiting, I soon realized that I was having trouble with the prism2 driver and setting a WEP key using the Linux command for managing wireless devices, iwconfig. We went back to COMPUSA the next day and I dropped another $60USD on a Netgear PCMCIA card that, thankfully, had an Atheros chip-set radio in it. This used the Madwifi driver and gave me the ability to connect to an encrypted network. I could now attack the AP with the PRISM2 card and attach to the network with the Atheros-based card. Too bad the machine only had one PCMCIA slot so I had to keep switching back and forth between devices. Needless to say, I became very familiar with the PCMCIA controller commands.

One day, while sitting on the tan carpeted stairs leading up to the second floor of my apartment, I was following along with Christophe Divine's WEP cracking flash video and jamming to the German song about Moscow. It took me a few attempts but I finally was able to inject ARP, or Address Resolution Protocol packets[6] into my WiFi network and see the replies in the 802.11 protocol analyzer Airodump.[7] Airodump would "listen" on the specific channel my radio was "set" to for any wireless traffic. I stopped Airodump and restarted it to write a cap, or packet capture, file. I also started Aircrack on the cap file as its size grew from my fake traffic. It took about half a million injected packets or so, but I was ultimately able to crack my 40 bit WEP key. *Holy Shit!* This was incredible inspiration. I remember getting chills. I remember the sweet lapse of intense awe. My mind and heart were racing. My fingers flew across the keyboard shooting commands into the Bash shell and I wanted to tell everyone I knew online about it.

This was yet another life changing event and how this book's story unfolds.

---

[6] ARP packets are used to find out who (identified by the MAC address) has what IP address.
[7] This was not the current "ng" version back then.

Ch☠pter 2 - Sea Skiddy

I now spent most of my nights cracking the WEP key of my router, resetting it to something else, then, cracking it again. My practice was on repeat and I was randomly setting my WEP keys. I was learning with hands on experience how to make the packet injection process go quicker and smoother, advanced security features of my router's firmware, and how WEP worked. I realized that I could generate an ARP request using my silver "phat" Nintendo DS by using Animal Crossing and opening the gates of my town for visitors. To add to this, hands on experience, I was also learning also about the Dsniff Suite and Fragrouter. I was performing advanced man in the middle attacks and learning how to leech files from my unprotected Windows shares all within the comfort of RF waves. I was even completely capable of brute forcing my router's password and thought about how lame it was that I could make so many attempts without any security in the router trying to slow me down or stop me. Most of my days were spent with my nose in the terminal now, or online learning as much as I could about WiFi security and advanced network device enumeration. I was watching flash videos and contributing my thoughts and test results to forums and on IRC channels.

Reading through the packets of my wardriving scans using packet analyzing software called Wireshark,[8] I was able to learn much more than average skiddy about what actually happened during wireless transactions. At the same time, I felt invisible. I was the ghost in the ether, so to speak. I could do all of these things with WiFi and who would catch me?

It was about this time, when I obtained my first copy of 2600 magazine. I joined their IRC, or internet relay chat, network and channel under the alias "Seadog." I read every issue from there on, cover to cover. I downloaded all of the videos and mp3's of the HOPE, or "Hackers on Planet Earth," conference. I even listened to the radio show Off the Hook with Emmanuel Goldstien. My other personal podcasts to listen to were the Phonelosers of America podcast and Default radio with Decoder and Lucky225. The history of hacking really grabbed my attention as well. I stumbled upon Evan Doorbell's phone trip recordings and listened to them on my iPod. I bought "Freedom Downtime" on DVD and found Kevin Mitnick's web site. There was so much information freely available online about the subject that I was in constant overtime and without sleep. I was immersing myself in the new word I had found. My hobbies branched off to other hacker activities from the new things I was hearing and reading. I started picking simple door handle locks and learning about physical security too. Eventually, I joined the Phone Losers of America forums and started soldering phone phreaking boxes, social engineering and exploring the boxes on telephone poles and underground Bell cans. There was such a lack of security in the phone system and internet that I literally started to see the world differently.

During any of this learning and hacking, I still knew very little about all of it. I was constantly backtracking to relearn algebra, calculus, and all the while my Perl programming skills were getting much stronger. I was moving away from system calls and using Perl modules and actual logic. All of the magazines, forums posts, and websites I frequented all stated that the knowledge should be used to better the

---

[8] Wireshark was called "Ethereal" back then.

security world and not for malicious intent. Well, most of the time they did anyway. I felt this was the case, but, I too desired to know things behind closed doors, curtains, and the mask. Sometimes, I just had to know.

I once remember being at a party in my brother's apartment, drinking beer and sitting with my laptop in his living room. I was scanning with Airodump for APs and was watching the power levels. If the power level was high enough for me to attempt to crack its security, I tried to crack it. The first one I found, I cracked almost instantly. It took less than 300,000 packets to get the 40bit WEP key. I recognized the key as a local phone number that started with 412. This gave me chills and goose bumps. I felt a slight boost in energy. I cracked another and it too was only 40bit. I always used the '-n 64' flag in Aircrack first, because if the key were 40bit, it would crack it with fewer packets. Sometimes, if I set the fudge-factor up higher, I could crack the key faster too.

I jumped out of my seat and walked through a long hallway to his kitchen for more beer. As I walked, I felt taller. I felt proud. So, why was I feeling the physical and mental stimulation from simply hacking into a "secured" network? Well, because I actually *hacked* something. I knew I would have to do something far more 31337 to one day actually be called a hacker though and that wouldn't be for years from now. Hackers are incredibly smart. Most are on par with engineers and mathematicians. Cracking WiFi security was just an easy way into the network. In reality, nothing a hacker does is easy.

Wireless network penetration and hacking is a well-defined skill. I consider it an "art," if you will. It's not something one can master using only his resources and reading books. No. He needs to get out there and get real hands on training, in an organic, public setting. In the computer security field, the term "script kiddie" refers to a person who only uses scripts or programs to "crack" some form of security. No knowledge is required for the skiddy, or "script kiddy," he just downloads the file and executes it with his cannons pointed at the target. Most script kiddies work in an aimless, ballistic fashion, attacking everything they can until they get lucky. This was true about me back then, I admit, but to a good investment; I was gaining knowledge about routers, switches and other network devices, that I never would have with just my simple resources. I also, didn't work with a group or tell anyone about my hacking. I kept all of it to myself. This aimless hacking fueled my curiosity enough to keep me studying on the subject of wireless communications. *I realized that we are literally living in a sea of RF, or radio frequency waves, from baby monitors, WiFi, cellular communication, music radio, police radio, Bluetooth, and even microwaves.*[9]

I started a file of WEP keys, ESSID, or network names, and BSSID, or MAC address of the wireless router's radio, that grew pretty fast. I was aiming my radio promiscuously at any and every WEP encrypted router I found. I was testing new antennas and also learning on how to hardware-hack my equipment into performing differently.

One night at work, I had my laptop on the back table opened and scanning the air for APs. I usually worked the night shift with one other person. This time, it was a girl who made a deal with me. Ally and I would take turns helping the customers when it would slow down and the person in the back would sit at the table and relax. When it was my turn to sit in the back, I sat down at my machine and saw a router with the ESSID hidden. This Subway was in a strip mall with a few other businesses, restaurants and a bank two doors down. I wonder who would set this network up and try to hide it? Hiding the ESSID was such a lame excuse for network security. All this did was replace the ESSID value in the packets with null bytes. Anyone with a

---

[9] All of the above devices emit radiation (RF) in the ISM Band – ISM being Industrial Scientific and Medical spectrum which ranges from 2.400-2.500 for WiFi enabled devices. Microwaves "leak" a small amount within this band unintentionally at a much higher power (1500w vs WiFi < 1w).

amazon.com

	Item Price	Total
e	$17.49	$17.49
	$13.37	$13.37
		$30.86
		$3.98
		$34.84
		$34.84
		$0.00

V3

DMn2VKgvN/-2 of 2-/std-n-us/7693640 CVG5

Your order of February 16, 2013 (Order ID 103-5865405-6361863)

Qty.	Item
1	**Captive Audience: The Telecom Industry and Monopoly Power in the New Gilde** Crawford J.D., Susan P. --- Hardcover **(** ** A-10 ** **) 0300153139**
1	**Raiding the Wireless Empire** Berdeaux, Douglas --- Paperback **(** ** A-10 ** **) 1456587374**

Subtotal
Shipping & Hand
Order Total
Paid via credit/d
Balance due

This shipment completes your order.

Have feedback on how we packaged your order? Tell us at www.amazon.com/packa

true 802.11 protocol analyzer, like Airodump would see the management and control frames with null bytes where the network name would be. In fact, the protocol analyzer can see how many null bytes are used and determine the length of the hidden ESSID. When a client would connect to the AP it would have to send the ESSID a couple of times to the AP in plain text. In the 802.11 protocol for wireless communication, management and control frames are all unencrypted, which I use to my advantage. In these classes of packets were disassociation frames, which were used to sever a wireless connection between a host and its client by removing its NIC[10] entry from the association index. I could forge and send these to the network devices and client computers, which happily accepted them!

Every now and then, I noticed that a client machine would send a packet or two to the AP, so I decided to inject a de-authentication attack to the client machine forcing it to reconnect and send the ESSID in plain text while doing so. This action returned the name "hide_NC" which most likely stood for the initials of the bank! *Whoa, I gotta hack this!* It was around 6 in the evening and no one would be in the bank now. Plus, even if they were, no one would know I was hacking them! I spoofed my MAC address and locked onto the channel with the protocol analyzer. I tried a fake association and authentication attack on the router, but these failed. So, I unplugged the laptop and took it to the back door. The signal strength in Airodump was getting stronger. I kicked open the door with my foot, propped it open with a bucket of paint, and walked out into the back of the strip mall and down closer to the bank. Now, the signal was strong enough to perform the attack. I set the laptop down onto a garbage can and let it replay the ARP packet I caught while the client machine was communicating with the AP.

I eventually cracked its WEP key, which again was a phone number. I searched for it using Google and sure enough, it was the bank next door. I spoofed my phone number using a prepaid card and called the number. I realized from the voicemail that it was to the cubical or

---

[10] Network Interface Card

office of the bank manager, who would regularly come into the Subway and order food during the week. I lit a cigarette and my coworker came to the back door. I instantly flipped open my cell phone from my pocket and acted like I was on the phone with my mother and motioned to Ally that I would be back in, in a few minutes. She reluctantly went back into the restaurant to take my turn at the Subway counter. After which, I spoofed my MAC address, yet again, and connected to the AP. The sky above me was a nice dark blue as the sun was setting and filled with random clouds. Every now and then I would catch the scent of the garbage can my laptop was on, and had to turn my head away for a moment. I ran an Ettercap scan from the command line that returned fourteen hosts. *Wow, there's really direct access to the machines in the bank? I didn't even know there were 14 computers in there! Why would a WiFi router be routed to access those machines? Kinda stupid.*

Next, I ran an smbtree scan for SMB, or Small Message Block Windows shared directories, and found quite a few. I started to think that this was a rogue access point, put in by the bank manager so that he could have wireless access to the network with his laptop. I mounted all of the shares, which weren't password protected, and began leeching everything I could. All of the practice I had at home and from random APs paid off on this hack. This was my first illegal attack against a business network and my blood was pumping. I felt a slight swelling in my ears and my breathing changed. I was scared! All I could think about was reading through this material when I get home after work tonight.

While I was watching the leeching laptop's screen, I put out my cigarette on the ground and stepped back to get some fresher air. I leaned my head back and took a deep breath looking up at the sky again. This time, I noticed a small security camera on the back of the bank building near the roof pointing directly down at me! *Shit!* I pulled down my Subway visor and slapped the lid of the Pirate Ship closed sprinting back into the back room of the Subway restaurant, leaving the back door propped open. When I got in, I dropped the computer down onto the desk and just stood still. Now, my heart was really racing. I thought about how stupid it would have been if an ambulance had to come to the restaurant because I thought my panic attack was a heart attack. *Fuck.* Just then, my coworker came into the back and yelled "Your turn, slacker!"

I somehow made my way out to the counter and just stood there facing the storefront window in deep thought holding two plastic gloves. *I need to get back to that AP and destroy all the logs. I need to not give the bank any reason to check that camera. I need to wipe the camera feed. Hrmm. What if I..* Someone had walked into the store and up to the counter looking up at the menu and asked me to get Ally. It was her boyfriend. He came to visit her often and she never let him into the back of the store, so she gladly took my turn yet again and told me I look flushed. I thanked her and ran back to the laptop. I started a shred session on the bank directory I made for the leeched files to zero out all bits and remove any evidence of the Pirate Ship even being in those waters.

I then ran outside to the garbage can and connected back to the AP making sure to play the camera's view with my visor. I tried putting the router's IP address into the browser and was greeted with the login screen. The first default password and user name combination I tried failed and I noticed this was a Linksys router. I fired up HTC Hydra and tested the user name "admin" with my giant dictionary file. This failed too. *How? My word list is huge!* Then I decided to try the phone number that was the WEP key. This worked! *How could anyone be so stupid? I mean, this is a bank for shit's sake.* I clicked through the administration tabs and noticed that the AP logged a few HTTP requests to Gmail and remembered it was on my browser's homepage. *Stupid! Stupid! Stupid!* I deleted all of the logs I could find in the system. After messing around with it, I restarted the router and didn't log back into it.

That night when I was at home, I was sitting on one of the many computers laying on the floor in deep thought. I was glancing all around the room at my things and wondering what someone would do with it all if I died or went to prison. I looked at the Pirate Ship and thought about giving up my adventures. *Maybe I would just cool it down a bit on the black hat[11] stuff?*

The anxiety, as it usually did, only took a good night's sleep to wear off completely. The next morning, I told a few of my friends about the adventure and wouldn't tell them which bank it was, so that they wouldn't do anything stupid. I changed my browser's configuration to open a blank page as its home page to avoid that stupidity again and made sure no services were "phoning home," so to speak so that nothing could be traced back to me in the future, when I may not be so lucky as to get full administration access to the WiFi router I was hacking.

---

[11] Black Hat - most of the time, "evil doer hacker."

Chapter 3 - Should Have Been Last Call

About a year later, WHAX! And Auditor Linux went through a few changes and combined. The sum was called BackTrack Linux which I had installed on the Pirate Ship. There was a little support for Broadcom chip-set radios by this time, but nothing functional to the point of being able to hack with it. I opened up the D-Link PCMCIA WiFi adapter and modded it to have a larger external antenna. I also acquired a cheap Bluetooth device that I used to query Bluetooth enabled phones and devices, most of which had barely any known vulnerabilities by now.

I was now working for a cellular carrier as a sales associate in a large kiosk in a mall. I was ecstatic to realize that I was permanently done with handling food as my primary job. Sometimes the mall was quiet, especially in the mornings when old folks would lap the building for exercise. Employees would be pulling up their gates and counting and their registers. The smell of baked and fried fast food filled the air. I would load up on caffeine and the mid-day rush wasn't for several hours after the mall opened. This gave me enough space to study. I only had a high school diploma and never had any of the advanced mathematics or physics courses that I was into now. When I was in high school, I wasted a lot of time as a complete idiot and slacker. I just simply couldn't take anything seriously for the life of me. As I said before, I am very influenced by media and back then I listened to anarchy themed music. So, I now spent most of my free time at the store again reading calculus, trigonometry, and physics books. Sometimes when my friends would ask why I was studying, I wasn't sure why, but my brain was like a dried, thirsty sponge. I was bored with life. I stopped drinking a while ago, I didn't party or socialize much, and I never went anywhere. But, damn, I loved opening up a notebook and following along with the text books!

I also fell in love with Quantum Mechanics. The books I read and videos I watched on the subject hooked me instantly. One day, my girlfriend talked me into getting tattoos with her and, of course, mine was really nerdy. It was a physics tattoo written in *1337* and had a diagram of an LED schematic I obtained from an index-able Apache server hosted by MIT and an equation for the energy of a subatomic particle. *I never would have thought that this tattoo would save my ass one day.*

As my days were spent working my neurons to the bone, my nights were spent with mischievous hacking and urban exploring. I still climbed telephone poles, fences, walls, picked locks of cell tower gates and telco equipment, climbed down into Bell cans, beige boxed, red boxed, blue boxed, dove into dumpsters for documents and even hid in bushes, trees, or on garages while using someone's "secured" WiFi to IRC, or run Nmap and scan IP blocks. One night, I finally talked my brother into phone phreaking with me. I packed a black laptop bag full of equipment and cables. We dressed in all black and made our way down into the city using public transportation. The night was chilly and we walked aimlessly through alleys and down streets. The city was pretty much dead after 8p.m. on the weekend. Every now and then we would peek into a dumpster in hopes that we would find some computer equipment.

We made our way to the north shore of Pittsburgh and found a secluded telephone pole that had rungs low enough to reach. I flipped the bag of equipment onto my back and started to climb up. When I got to the top, I reached out and clicked open the terminal box using my right arm. Just then, a swarm of wasps fell straight down out of the box. "Bees!" I yelled, and climbed down two rungs or so before dropping the equipment bag and jumping down. When I landed I sprained my wrist, but made it back to the earth without a single wasp sting. We waited back away from the pole for a few minutes before going back for the bag.

Later we stumbled upon a Pizza Hut restaurant and decided to check the back of the store for a TNI, or Telephone Network Interface, box. Sure enough one was there. I had built a wireless beige box that was connected to a DC battery and decided to use it, so that I could play with their phone line from a distance. The shop was still open at the time. I unscrewed the box with the torque wrench from the bag and pulled it open. "No bees." I said as we laughed. I attached the alligator clips to the terminals and disconnected one from the line going into the building so that they wouldn't hear the phone ring when a customer called. I closed the box over and left the bag on the ground underneath it. We walked back towards the grassy unkempt hill behind the restaurant and I pulled the rubber band off of the handset releasing the mute button. I turned the phone on and heard the dial tone. Oh such a sweet, heartwarming sound the dial tone is when you are on the field, phreaking at night.

I had rewired the handset microphone and earpiece into a grey terminal box that I had taped onto the back of it with exposed terminals and an emergency kill switch. I also soldered on 2.5mm headphone port which I used to record the calls with a small battery powered Radio Shack recording device. After settling down behind a garbage can in some weeds, I turned on the recorder and waited for customers to call. I had the ringer turned off and removed from the base station, which was nestled in the TNI box on the back of the building. When a call would come I would see the LED's on the handset blinking and answer.

After the first call, I thought it would be funny to setup call forwarding to a different pizza shop and flipped open my phone to use it's limited and extremely slow internet connection to find the number of a local shop. After a minute of waiting around, a car pulled around to the back of the building with its headlights off. It was a police car! I felt my heart drop into my stomach. I was so scared. *Oh my god! What do I do?*

I casually dropped the handset into the tall grass and began walking toward the TNI to get the bag. He flipped on his headlights and overhead lights on the roof of his car. *I am so fucked.* He got out of the car and yelled at us instantly, asking us what the hell we were doing. At that instant, without any preparation at all, I came up with an incredible story about being a physics student and showed him the TNI[12] box that had the cordless phone base station set in it. I had modified it so much that it resembled a piece of space garbage from a Star Wars film. He looked at it in the light of his head lights. I told him I was a poor student that couldn't afford my own land line and I was developing a new type of phone system. I said I thought it wouldn't harm the business to use theirs when they weren't. He told us that we could go to federal prison for wiretapping, and attempting to burglarize the company. He also asked for ID and neither of us had any. Just then I decided to roll up my sleeve and show him my physics tattoo. I told him what it meant and how Planck's constant[13] meant so much to me that I just had to get it tattooed. He called us nerds and looked us both in the face back and forth for what felt like a whole minute. "You two better disappear, right now. Don't go using another phone line. If you are broke and a student, there are ways to get support from the government to help you. Just ask your school" he said. Then he handed me the black bag and base station. I reconnected the terminal back into the building so that Pizza Hut could receive incoming calls and closed up the TNI box with the torque wrench.

---

[12] Telephone Network Interface
[13] 6.626e-34J/s – Describes how a quantum action cannot take on any indiscriminate value – it must be of a single infinitesimally small amount.

I'm pretty sure I just confused the shit out of him. Thank hell I decided to get the damned tattoo and practiced social engineering for so long! I am guessing he didn't feel like bothering with paper work about a "crime" that he didn't fully understand. As we walked away I said "Wholly Shit! We just got away with a federal crime and we were caught RED HANDED!" "Yeah, that got out of hand." My brother replied. I flung the bag over my right shoulder and realized the handset I made was back in the bushes behind the restaurant. I slammed the base station on the ground. Pieces of it flew in every direction. "FUCK!" I yelled. My brother said that we just had an unlucky night. He said that the police just have an unfair advantage over us because of fear. The show COPS and movies always display the police getting away with brutality. He lightened up the situation by reminding me that we *did* get away and were free. We departed the city for home and called it a night.

Ch☠pter **4** - Geek Squad

O ne summer night, Ethermine challenged me to a bet. He was fed up with Best Buy. The high prices, lies that the incompetent sales associates and Geek Squad told, in store propaganda, over the top security and, above all, the annoying repetitive hammering he would endure from nosy sales associates while simply trying to browse the store was enough for him not to go back. He showed me random clips and reviews online about how shitty their deep roots of conducting business and ethics were. Once when he confronted a member of the Geek Squad about a mistake they made to his mother's computer, the guy actually responded to him by saying that all members of Geek Squad are MIT[14] graduates. They even once told his mother that her internet connection would be faster if she purchased a wireless router and let them install it for her. She had no wireless devices, at all. It sat as a useless node between her cable modem and computer. They even had the nerve to make the fucking ESSID "1800GeekSquad." *Is that Free advertising? I don't want their fucking spam in my wardriving scans.*

So, he bet me that I couldn't hack them. I smiled and took on the bet. I think he knew I could, he just wanted me to.

---

[14] Massachusetts Institute of Technology

That night, I scanned their sites and subdomains I found from Google dorks[15] for vulnerabilities. I found a few minor non-persistent XSS holes and after making a few calls got the name of the managers and district manager for the area. I was able to find most of them on LinkedIn and got some of their cellphone numbers which I fed to random phone bombing services online. I called a Best Buy and pretended to be another Best Buy manager in the area with one of the names I had acquired. I asked to speak with the Geek Squad technician and was very stern. I told him that he was "doing a great job" and asked him several questions about how they implemented security. I made up some bullshit story about how I was being interrogated by some bureaucrat above me in the food chain and he related. He told me about remote desktop, and how they shared resources to the floor models on a wireless LAN. I just acted like I had no idea what he was talking about and he fell for it completely. I couldn't actually get him to say certain things to me without me feeling as if he would think twice. For example, he just said his wireless networks were "password protected" and that the manager of the store was "usually always around." I ended the conversation very politely and thanked him for his time. I told him I was eager to meet him next time I was in the store. Now, let's test their "physical" security.

Around 12a.m. We pulled into the empty Best Buy parking lot and pulled up to a spot directly in front of the store. I had my Airodump-ng screen open and already locked onto the channel used by the wireless router called "GeekSquad." It took only about 5 minutes of us playing SDLJump[16] in Gnome before I was able to retrieve the key. "Look! It's 104 bit WEP!" I said as he leaned over to see the computer screen.

This actually makes sense in a business setting. It was 2008 now and

---

[15] Special strings that are recognized by the Google search engine for advanced querying.
[16] Amazingly addictive game where you play a small man in green pants that needs to jump up onto platforms as the screen scrolls upwards.

most businesses still used WEP, because most small devices used within the store, such as hand held scanners, demo units like the Nintendo DS, and more are not powerful enough to utilize WPA2 CCMP. About half of them didn't even have firmware that supports WPA either.

We both laughed and I re-spoofed my radio's MAC address. After I connected to the network, I instantly used Ettercap-ng to scan for live hosts. I started another Bash session and scanned for Windows SMB shares. At the time, I was using a thirteen inch white MacBook with a custom version of Ubuntu that I made installed on it and a Ralink based Linksys WiFi adapter. I was also using a Perl program I wrote called NetGh0st which basically rapidly raped a LAN[17] for all of its details such as, File shares, open ports and services, external IP adresses, ISP info, IP addresses of hosts, gateways, nameservers, and more. It was an extremely noisy scan, but it worked rather well when speed was an issue.

After a little bit of probing, I found a Windows share that hosted AVI files taken from security cameras! Some of them showed people opening packages, breaking or throwing products, stealing, using counterfeit checks and money, and even fights. I found pictures of the store before the recent remodeling, the lab that the Geek Squad used behind their counter, and I even found an ISO image of a boot CD they use for troubleshooting. I left most of it, but swiped a few of the videos to prove to a few IRC friends that I was there and for the lulz.

Ethermine's jaw dropped. It was like a scene right out of a cheesy hacker movie to him. A port scan returned port 5900, which is usually used for VNC, so, I connected to it. It required no password at all and I had full control over the machine. I laughed hysterically like a mad scientist as Ethermine took a picture of my screen with his iPhone. We looked at each other and I said "you do realize that you've lost

---

[17] Local Area Network – a personal network comprised of networking devices and computers.

the bet right?" I started up Notepad.exe and left them a nasty letter. I moved a lot of their items directly into the Recycling Bin and changed their wallpaper to a picture of a Mudkip[18] in front of a blue screen of death that I found online. I was able to see the stored passwords for a few websites in Firefox, but none of them still worked. I downloaded a zipped package of Nirsoft tools that I had cached on a compromised server as a zip file, unzipped them and ran each one. They revealed more usernames and passwords, product key information, and I even ran an "undelete" utility from RoadKil to see some things that were recently deleted. I even went into the computer management console and removed all logs. Then, I dropped the connection and grabbed the external WAN IP address.

"You want a back door?" I said, while looking at the computer screen. I started up Metasploit and created a simple executable file for Windows that would reverse connect through a proxy that I had online to my machine. "As soon as they run this, you will have full access to the machine," I said. As I was looking for a place to plant the Trojan, I noticed that Ethermine didn't answer me so I looked over and he was concerned about a few cars that were passing through the parking lot. "Uhh.. " He curled his lip with concern and decided that it would be wise to leave since we were sitting in the first parking spot, which was intended for handicapped people, with my laptop open and hijacking the Geek Squads equipment. Plus there were security cameras on the front of the building pointing down at our car. "No, no, let's just get the fuck outta here, I'm hungry as hell." He finally replied. I was a bit frustrated that we had to leave before I could even really hack into anything, but I sympathized with his concerns and we backed out of the parking lot completely in reverse trying to play the security camera angles to not catch his license plate.

---

[18] "So, I herd U liek Mudkipz" an popular Internet meme that surrounds a well known Pokemon character.

Chapter 5 - The Router Repeater (Part 1)

Thinking back on the hack I did at the bank, I still feel as if I could have really brought that place down using that single rogue AP. I completely got away with it, too. The security cameras were my only real concern. *So how could I do the same without the cameras ever seeing me? How could I be there, but invisible? Could I hack into a system and use its wireless adapter to hack into other networks and systems? No. There are too many variables and that would be a long shot. Plus when they saw the MAC address of one system attacking all of the other networks and systems, it would be over pretty fast. If I do it all with my laptop I wouldn't have enough battery power and would have to make multiple trips.*

Then, I got the idea of creating the router repeater. I would plant a multi-radio router somewhere in another strip mall and access it remotely from another machine already within the mall. This is going to take some creativity and serious skill to get going. First, I designed a small circuit board that transferred only 12VDC from a 48~50VDC line coming in from alligator clips. It only took a few resistors, the board, and some simple soldering. I then routed the 12VDC out from the board into a power cable that fit into the back of the router and made sure the polarization was correct. Now, I could leech power from a plain old telephone service line and power a router.

What about the weather? I have to weather proof this router so that it doesn't get damaged while outdoors on the phone pole. I could power it from an underground land line in a Bell can, but WiFi doesn't propagate through the earth very well and with that much attenuation, or signal loss, I would risk screwing up the whole hack. I covered the router in a black plastic box and made it look like an old telephone company owned piece of hardware.

Now, to test it, I climbed the post in an alley that I knew no one would drive down on a Sunday evening. Once up, I used my beige box to find a working pair of terminals. When I did, I connected the box and saw it light up. *Success!* I left the box on the post overnight and returned to see the signal is gone. This confused me. I ascended the pole, wrapped by belt around it, and opened my black box. All of the lights on the router where lit up. *Hrmm.* Any power spike wouldn't make it through the circuit board without destroying the resistors, which visibly looked fine. I descended and pulled my multimeter out of my back pack. I turned it to the continuity and tested the resistors which were all fine. After a couple of minutes of wondering what could have screwed up the router, I finally realized what it was; a phone call. *How dare they use their own phone lines for phone calls!?* If a phone call came through I bet it dropped the power of the router just enough to brown out the firmware from functioning properly.

I climbed the post and attached a long phone line to the working terminals and dropped the wire down to the ground. When I got to the ground I attached my beige box to it and dialed an ANAC, or automatic number announcement circuit. This returned the phone number. I hooked my router up to the cable and watched as it booted up. I scanned for the beacons with my laptop and saw it functioning just fine. Then I called the phone number with my cell phone. The lights got really bright on the front of the router then went dim.

That's it. I gently yanked the cable down from the pole and put all of the gear back into my back pack and walked back home in complete focus of how to avoid this problem.

I spent about a week installing different open sourced operating systems onto the router. It turned out that the version of Aircrack-ng compiled for the DD-WRT version of the OS worked best. It took only about 10 minutes of playing with Aircrack-ng to realize that I needed more ROM space for the PCAP, or packet capture, file. So, I used a USB drive in one of the routers USB ports. The whole time, I was wondering how I could build a failsafe feature into my circuit board. The only option I could come up with is to add a battery onto the board between the POTS, or plain old telephone service, line and the router connector. This seemed like a bit much and I was very eager to test this in the wild. Then, I realized that I could just stop calls from coming in on the line. Or, better yet, I could just wait till the weekend and use a business that is not open over the weekend. Luckily, there was an insurance company in the plaza that was closed all weekend. Usually this annoyed the hell out of me. If I worked all week long during normal business hours, then how the hell could I ever do business with these people. So I felt a slight irony and bit of vengeance as I used their line. That is where and when I will perform my attack.

The next Friday night, Ethermine dropped me off at the bus stop in the plaza around midnight. There were still a few cars lingering in the parking lot so I just put in my ear bud headphones and curl up on the bus stop bench dozing off while listening to VNV Nation. When I woke up my hands were severely freezing and all of the cars were gone, but out of the corner of my eye I noticed the security guards SUV pulling around from the back of the plaza making his rounds. I would have to time this perfectly to not be detected and I wanted to wait and warm up my hands. I pulled a hand warming pack from my backpack and opened it. As it started to warm up I could feel my hands thanking me. I sprinted down the hill and into the back of the plaza. This reminded me of an assassin themed video game. I was going to wait until he drove all the way around to climb the pole and mount the device. There were lights on the back of the building that would surely give me away if he drove around while I was up there.

I hid in the trees behind the driveway in the back of the plaza and put my hand warmer into my back pocket. I saw his headlights as he pulled around from the front of the plaza and drive down the small road. Every store he went past he stopped his truck to get out and test the back doors of the stores *to make sure they were closed. I hope.* When he went back around to the front of the plaza I jumped down and ran directly towards the pole. I lifted my leg up and almost ran up the first 5 feet of the pole from the ground grabbing onto the rungs. Once I was up, I attached three long wires on the first three sets of terminals in the box and let them fall to the ground. I felt the hand warmer in my back pocket on the side of my ass and snickered. I then descended and grabbed all three cables and through them around the pole so they wrapped around. I then fed them back into the bushes behind the pole and took off my back pack, throwing it into the bushes. I pulled out a yeti blanket and covered myself while I tested the three lines with the beige box. None of which were the insurance company. *Dammit.* I waited close to ten minutes before he came back around the plaza from the front and then waited again for him to return. I jumped up and left all the wires there. I ascended and reattached the three cables to the next three terminal pairs. I climbed down and repeated this until I found the Insurance company's phone lines by making simple calls to an ANAC.[19]

By this time, the security guard had sat idle in his truck in the front of the plaza for about twenty five minutes or so and I just took the risk of being out in the open. After yanking down the other two cables and wrapping them around my arm in a loop, I climbed the post and mounted the router on the insurance company's pair. I let the last cable fall before descending. After that, I shoved all of them and the

---

[19] Automatic Number Announcement Circuit – system that repeated back to you the phone number you were calling from.

yeti blanket back into my back pack and zipped it up.

After standing still in thought about how to proceed, walked back into the wooded area and set up a small camp. I climbed a tree right next to me and mounted my 7dbi WiFi panel antenna and 1W ALFA radio, aiming it directly at the back of the plaza. A few weeks before, I used a sharpie to color over the green LED on the back of the radio to dim it a little. Then, I attached a 25 foot active USB cable and let it drop down. When I climbed down, I plugged it into the laptop. I made sure I dimmed the screen as much as possible and laid stomach down on the ground with the yeti blanket over me, so that I just looked like a pile of leaves.

I scanned and found all of the wireless networks from the plaza. One of them had WEP and was for a famous woman's cosmetics store. *This looks good.* I cracked the 40bit WEP in just under 5 minutes and attached to the network. I scanned for clients and found three. I fired up the `msfconsole` utility from the Metasploit Framework and performed a port scan and remote exploitation attack on a Windows XP machine running a Windows share. I gained access to the system via a simple meterpreter shell and uploaded some executable files for password recovery and back dooring.

The next step was to run a few simple DOS commands and I obtained the external IP address to the cosmetics store, which I typed into a vim window. Next, I have to attack the router to get administrative access. I started a THC Hydra attack and found the password after about 10 minutes. What I did was write a simple Perl application that mangled an input word in many ways, by changing case, adding in numbers, and so on. It turned out that the password was just the default value of "administrator," I just had it as an entry deep in my wordlist for some reason. After I was in, I added port forwarding to the hacked machine running the Cygwin SSH server and the port number I specified. Then, I added external WAN access to the router. Since I already had the password, I wouldn't have to change it. I tested the SSH server by logging in from the external WAN IP address and it worked. *Done.* I stood up and threw all of my equipment back into my backpack after retrieving the WiFi radio from the tree branches above. I walked out into the back of the plaza onto the small road and started walking towards the bus stop.

When I got back home, I looked through a list of Linux based web servers that I had access to from LFI, SQL injection, or other remote exploits. One that stuck out to me was in the states, so I started an SSH session to it using the neighbor's "protected" wireless access point. From there, I started an SSH session to the cosmetics store. I started the netsh.exe shell and attached the wireless adapter in the machine to my hidden access point behind the store. It took some effort and a bit of Googling, but the machine now routed between the LAN to the WAN and now out to the LAN on the router outside. The next thing I did was start cracking the WEP and WPA encryption keys of the nearby networks that reside in the plaza, using only my hidden wireless router. There were only two that had WPA enabled. Once I got the handshakes from them, I brought them all the way home using SCP. From the router, they went to the cosmetics store machine. From there, they went to another hacked private web server. Then I used Tor and downloaded them to my machine via the neighbor's WAN connection. From home, I performed offline dictionary attacks using Pyrit over night. My laptop at this time had an amazing internal NVIDIA graphics card and I was using Pyrit to generate massive rainbow tables. These tables were simply hashes using the ESSID, or broadcast name of the wireless router and every word in a 5GB word-list file. This made the process of "cracking" a password as easier by doing all the work ahead of time. If several routers had the same ESSID, like "linksys" for example, then I could use the same rainbow table to attempt to crack each router. I would often wrap my laptop in plastic bags with a hole in the side where the fan blew out. Then I would place the system in the freezer to keep maximum performance while crunching the wireless WPA and WPA2 passwords.

Before the end of the weekend, I had gained access to most systems in the plaza from the comfort of my own computer room at home. I had SSH and meterpreter shells, VNC sessions, remote access to the router's administration panels, and much, much more. Similar to the fashion in which I downloaded the WPA handshakes from the router to my local machine, I did the same to every Windows shared directory I found in the plaza. I was passing the shares to systems I had VNC access to and zipping the huge files up for departure. It took a lot of patience and caffeine to help my attention span through this part of the process.

At the time, this was a huge hack for me. I ended up just skimming through some of the data and then using shred on it all after saving any credentials I found. One of the machines in which I had no administrative rights to, I was forced to leave the logs intact. I had no real motive to do this kind of hack, but to just see if I could.

One night after work, I walked over to the plaza, climbed the pole and retrieved the router repeater before making my way to the bus stop.

Chapter **6** - Digital Love and Digital Hate

Part I: Meeting People Is NOT Easy

Through the few years I spent learning computer security, I would like to think that I became more imaginative in my wireless hacking and exploits. I loved playing simple tricks on people and exploring the world using bleeding edge software and hardware. I was also coding a lot of fun things myself now. I started my own security distribution of Linux to use within the small lab in my home. I showed a few people and they asked me to upload it for them to use too. I built it from Ubuntu at first, but eventually moved my custom kernel and code over to Debian Linux. After some time, I coded a small web page and started giving it out to everyone online.

Needless to say, I was spending mostly all of my free time now writing code to satisfy all of the new requests or constantly troubleshooting issues. One tool I was working on was called "WiFiCake-ng." This was simply a Perl-Tk[20] front end application that used the Aircrack-ng

---

[20] Perl Tk is a set of instructions and libraries of instructions for writing graphical user interface code with windows – as opposed to command line programming.

Suite, Pyrit, and it made PDF format reports of the penetration tests. Sometimes, I liked to write code in public places where no one knew me and I could concentrate better. Coffee shops were nice because of the caffeine and constant flow of people that wouldn't notice me lingering all day.

One Saturday morning, I got up early, threw my equipment into my bag and took the bus down to a coffee shop in the south side of Pittsburgh called "Beehive." It wasn't a bad place. The people who frequented it looked interesting. I would overhear conversations about the end of the world because of economic collapse, pollution, and politics. People scattered around the large place and sometimes sat around in large groups. I was drawn to the place because of the "Free WiFi" sign hanging in the front window. I got there early and setup on a table in one of the empty rooms after purchasing a large soda. I was using a DELL laptop at this point, which I always carried in a large backpack that was stuffed full of wireless equipment. Antennas, GPS units, connectors, tools, lock picks, medicine, and even some food. Maybe I too was preparing for a post-apocalyptic life? Now my thoughts were focused on coding. I was sniping off errors and testing WiFiCake-ng. My brain was a train and I was coding away making substantial progress at this point. After about a half an hour or so, the place started to fill up with some people and one of them was an odd looking but sort of cute girl that sat directly across from me. I couldn't help but to notice her tattoos and scowl as she pulled out her laptop and aimed it right across the tables at mine. She looked as if she really didn't want to be there and sighed as she fell into her seat holding in the power button on the laptop. *What the hell is her problem?* Pulling out a notebook and college text book from her bag, she began taking notes and reading her computer screen. Now, I could only see the top of her face and head. Her hair was pulled back tightly and her eyes were dark as her screen cast a slight glow on her puckered up face. It almost looked as if she were trying to translate a language she didn't know. I couldn't tell if she was in a bad mood, or was just born pissed.

After slowly declining into unproductivity, I couldn't concentrate. I sat back and sighed taking a few sips of my soda and looking around the room at the other people around us. I noticed a guy sitting a few tables over that had some gaming stickers plastered on the top of his computer who looked like he really didn't give a shit about having a massive amount of hair or any personal hygiene. I told myself that I had to focus and pulled back into my laptop resting my hands upon the keys and my eyes on the open vim window. *Urg, I really* couldn't think about the software I was writing. I started to think about the girl across from me and why she looks so pissed. *What was she there for? Does she not have internet at home? What was she studying, disgusting gore films? What kind of things did she have on her computer?* Every now and then, she caught me looking up at her and our eyes would meet just as I would look down at my computer. After day dreaming for five or ten minutes, the rest of the people scattered and left the room. Now, it was just her and I. *Should I go over and talk to her? What the hell would I even say? "I hope your day gets better?" No, that's lame. Just finish the software and focus.*

Instantly after those thoughts, I had an idea. I started a Bash shell and browsed into my wireless hacking tools directory. I started a VAP, or virtual access point, in promiscuous mode on my WiFi radio device and dropped my connection to the wireless access point. Then I opened up GIMP, or Gnu Image Manipulation Tool, and made a plain image with words on it. The image said "Hey, the guy sitting across from you thinks you have a nice computer. You look mad. Need help with your homework?" Then I started AirPWN and let it fly after making sure my WiFi adapter was locked onto the same channel as the AP labeled "beehive." AirPWN would change all of her image requests to anything I chose in HTTP requests made via the WiFi connection. If she browsed to, say, Google Image Search, AirPWN would alter her packets going to and from the wireless access point to point to my image.

Was this invasive? Naw. It's her fault for breaking my concentration and being cute. She was writing in her notepad on the table next to her laptop. Every now and then, I saw her scroll down on the page she was reading on her screen. I waited watching the AirPWN session for output patiently.

After what felt like five minutes, the AirPWN session showed her request a few images and attempting to alter the packets. Bingo! It looked as if she ignored it as ads, but after another minute or two I saw her expression finally change and head come up as she straightened her slouch. She didn't look pissed! Success! I put my head down into my screen and smiled widely. I turned my head to the wall to avoid her from seeing me and I felt what only could be described as my brain being sucked out of my ear! I had accidentally pulled out my ear bud headphone from my right ear as my arm moved. The ear bud hit my keyboard and I heard it make a loud slapping sound. *Shit!* I knew my face was now beet red. I casually pulled the left ear bud out of my ear and turned back towards my computer screen. *Why the fuck did that have to happen right now? Really?*

As I looked up, she was already standing next to me holding her computer! My heart dropped into my stomach as I looked up at her. Now with a closer look at her, I noticed that she was an attractive girl minus the tattoos. I couldn't help but release a huge smile on my face, which changed her scowl to a smile too. "Hey." she said. "Heya. Uh. Hi there." I responded as I laid my other ear bud on the laptop keys. "Did you do something to my computer? Did you hack me?" She asked, still smiling. Her smile was nice and her voice was soft, but her words sounded forced. "No, I was just sniffing and playing around with your packets, as a prank." I said. "Ooh, that sounds naughty," she said jokingly, after which, she asked to sit with me. "Mind if I sit?" "No, go ahead. I'm Seadog, by the way." I responded to ease some of the awkwardness that still lingered. She sat her laptop down and walked back to her table to grab her other things turning her head back at me saying "I'm Jamie, nice to meet you." I couldn't help but just hope that she wasn't a hipster. So far, it was good.

After an awkward introduction and small talk I began to tell her about how AirPWN works. She was barely intrigued by any of it, I could tell, and put on a pair of thick framed glasses. She was a student at the University of Pittsburgh and was actually doing research on an activist group that she told me all about. This, I liked. Unfortunately, we talked for only a few minutes after that before she started mentioning shit that only jaded hipsters would fess up to. Their culture is so annoying to me. I started to realize her glasses were just clear plastic lenses that weren't real and that I wasn't listening to her words as much. I started thinking about the software I was writing and what other coffee house I would plant my productivity to avoid this. I gave humanity too much faith yet again. After a while, I mentioned that I was about to leave before we started talking and politely departed. When I left she was smiling, so I guess I was able to use hacking to at least steer her day in a good direction.

P☠rt II: Economy Induced Whiplash

Sometime after that incident, I was having a difficult time making financial ends meet. It was hard to make good commission at a job I hated and by slacking off and reading text books. I really couldn't have cared less about selling or repairing cellphones anymore. Sometimes, as I would study, people would walk past my kiosk and yell vulgar remarks at me if they saw me studying. Why the hell would anyone make fun of another person while they were studying? At this point, I was beginning to think the movie Idiocracy was a true story that just had not happened yet.

This sucked. My bills were high from my servers and I wasn't making a single dollar from my software or security lab. I had a lot of health issues I couldn't resolve from having a low income no benefits job.

Out of all of my bills, I realized that my cable bill was outrageous when considering the amount of downtime I endured. *Dark times call for desperate measures. The economy sucks, I'm tired of waiting around wasting time, and I have to do something to survive.* I canceled my cable service and sent their shitty modem back to the ISP. I was going buy a bigger antenna and just leech internet from my richer neighbors.

I knew which network was theirs because they made the ESSID their last name plus the word "house." Go figure. I really didn't mind leeching. First of all, I never hacked from home. Secondly, I never hacked for profit. But, I don't torrent anything or stream movies in HD. I only really use the internet late at night browsing /b/ or chatting on IRC, so I am pretty sure they wouldn't even notice.

The neighbors had Fios, or Fiber Optic service, which was much faster and more reliable than my cable connection. I cracked the WEP key almost in seconds. When I accessed the network, I browsed to the web administration interface to access the router. It was an Actiontec router and the interface displayed the ISP as Verizon.

If I were to use the network, I would need full access to the router for port forwarding and clearing the logs. On the next garbage night, around 3am or so, I stole all of their garbage bags and put them on my back deck. After spending about thirty minutes rummaging through, I found a lot of good information on my target. I then put all of the trash back into new garbage bags and plopped them back in front of the neighbor's house, hoping they wouldn't notice.

Later that night, I tested all of the known default passwords from the CIRT website and even tested the default password that the Verizon techs used. None of them worked. I started THC Hydra and let it go for every word list I could find. I even tried my program that added numbers and letters, spliced words, and changed the case randomly. Nothing worked. I looked them up in the phone book online and tested their phone numbers. I tried their names, children names and even their address. I was just out of luck.

The next night, around 11p.m. or so, I noticed that the access point wasn't on. I instantly thought they knew I was leeching from them. I was tired and gave up for the night. In the morning before heading out to work, I noticed that the access point was back up and running with my Android phone. I tested the WEP key and it was still the same. *Why did it go off last night? What the hell?* I opened my laptop and connected to the network. After which I started Wireshark and Ettercap-ng to forward all packets from the entire internet network through my system and sniff them.

When I got home about nine hours later I had a huge amount of data waiting for me. I searched through the packets using Wireshark and found some HTTP cookies which I set into my browser using a Firefox plugin. I was then able to log into one of their FaceBook accounts. After doing more research, I deleted the massive packet capture file and cookies. I now had enough information on the family to perform a simple social engineering attack on the ISP.

After spoofing my phone number to theirs, I called Verizon. I seriously had to jump through hoops in their PBX, or private branch exchange phone system, to get a technical support representative on the phone. When I did, I used the "I am extremely illiterate, but really polite" technique on the representative and was able to provide all of the information he asked for, which was actually just the address, city and state name, and zip code! After which, I asked the guy if he could "reset the password on my internet cellyair machine." When he realized I meant "wireless router" he gave me some information on the router, which meant he had remote access to it.

He told me the ESSID, WEP key, and that "I" had changed the password for the "admin" user, which was usually the serial number on the bottom of the unit. He also said he couldn't reset the password for me. *Dammit.* He told me the only thing he could do is "hard reset" the router. He also said that he couldn't tell me which ports where being forwarded to where. With the technician on the phone with me, my fingers flew across my laptop and I started a man in the middle attack on all machines on the LAN again. I port scanned the router for opened ports and then tried to connect to the ports from the internet using Netcat by using the external WAN IP address. This showed me which port went to where and there were only three. *Easy enough.*

After blaming all of this on "my kids" I told him to go ahead and hard reset the router. It was late at night and I was already running a man in the middle attack which didn't show any traffic. When he said it was done, I was told the new ESSID, WEP key (which was the same), and the administrator password. I hung up the phone without saying thanks or goodbye. After connecting to the network and logging into the router I forwarded the ports to the hosts and changed the ESSID back to the neighbor's last name. I also changed the password and enabled external WAN access to it.

All was fine with my shiny new internet connection until the next night came along. I noticed a pattern. When the family would go out or to sleep they would sometimes turn the wireless router off. *What the fuck? Who does that?* So I continued putting up with it and ended up rooting my Android phone and using it for a 3g tethering device with Cyanogen's mod. This was slow and annoying. Why did they turn the router off all the time? I even imagined them flipping off a light switch that severed power to the wall outlet that powered the router without knowing. It was so annoying, that I even considered breaking into the neighbor's house and rewiring the router using extension cables. *Nah, too risky and stupid. This has gone too far.*

One night I was drunk. I had a shitty day at work being hassled by ghetto assholes who blamed me for their carelessness with their handsets. I decided that I was going to just space out and watch Hulu with my laptop using the neighbor's internet service. Then I thought about them turning off the router all the time and became furious. *Fuck Hulu.* I started another man in the middle attack and fired up

Lighttpd. Once this began, I browsed to my web server's root directory and opened index.html in a vim window. I made the page say:

"STOP TURNING OFF YOUR ROUTER AT NIGHT. WE OWN THE INTERNET. WE FUCKING OWN YOU, YOU PATHETIC MEATBAG. WE KNOW EVERYTHING ABOUT YOU MOTHER FUCKER. WE HAVE ALL YOUR INFORMATION. SO KNOCK IT OFF BEFORE WE DESTROY YOU"

Just below that, I placed a picture of a pirate wearing a Guy Fawke's mask that I had on my hard drive. Then I passed out on the desk.

The next day, I woke up around 1p.m. With a huge headache from the rum and my neck was stiff from sleeping at my desk. I looked at my screen and saw that the access point was gone again. *What the hell, man?* I then realized what I did the night before. I started Airodump-ng and noticed a *new* access point. It was theirs, I could tell by the BSSID, or MAC address of their access point's radio. *They must have gotten scared the night before and changed all of their settings. They probably called the ISP for help.* It was now protected with WPA2 CCMP and I was able to nab a handshake from de-authenticating one of their machines. *How was I going to go about cracking this?* I searched for word lists on the Pirate Bay and considered purchasing an Amazon EC2 system with CUDA capable GPUs to use Pyrit, but there's not much chance I would really get the pass phrase if they had help from the ISP. CUDA programming utilizes the GPU, or graphics processor unit, and device memory in parallel, spawning many threads, or tasks. This technology processes data far faster than a simple CPU processor. A simple CPU could do a single process very quickly, one at a time, whereas a CUDA capable GPU would do several at a time just a little bit slower and producing faster output. The code does this by instructing the CPU to hand off other tasks to the "device" (a graphics card usually) to process it and return the results back to the "host" or main computer. It was the best option at the time for cracking passwords using an offline dictionary attack, especially with the Pyrit application and WPA. I decided to make a wordlist from the information I had gathered at the start. I used my Perl application to manipulate every line multiple times. It was now at about one million words. I started up Aircrack-ng and tested it against the packet capture file that contained their handshake, using my new word list. My neck was killing me and I decided to nap.

When I woke up, hours later, Aircrack-ng had finished and I had no pass phrase. *What do I do? Oh, yeah, I could call the ISP and get them to help me! How Ironic.* After dialing the ISP and passing through their system, I got a technician to hard reset the router again, telling them my "fucking kids were playing around with it again."

At this point, I wasn't concerned with using this access point any longer and decided to make my message clear to the neighbors. I changed their ESSID back to the new name, turned off all encryption and port forwarding, and started up another Man in the middle attack which pointed all of the HTTP requests to my custom made web page which read:

"STOP FUCKING AROUND. DO NOT TURN OFF YOUR ROUTER, OR CHANGE THE PASSWORD. OR WE WILL SET IT ON **FIRE.** WE *ARE* WATCHING YOU"

This time I started Wireshark to view proof of them visiting the page. They will have to realize that their Windows computers will need to re-associate with the access point since I reset it without a WPA password. I laughed and let the machine go while I jumped into the shower. Later than night, the router was modified by the neighbors again and I noticed a police car in front of their house. This made me laugh as I unplugged my radio from the laptop. I ran up the street to a higher view of it and snapped a picture of their house and the police car with my phone.

Later that very night, I did the whole process yet again to try to gain access to their network. This time Verizon asked me for a security code. Shit. How do I get around that? I have an Idea. I called their house after spoofing my number to a support line 800 number that I found on Verizon's website. I told them I was with the security department and that I had made progress in finding the "bad guys responsible for doing this to their systems." The guy sounded eager and pissed off so he complied with everything I said. I asked him to confirm his security code so that I knew he wasn't one of the hackers and **he gave it to me**. I told him I was going to alter some of the software in his router "to help catch the hackers" and asked him his administrative password and WPA key. He gave them both to me, fully believing I was a Verizon technician. Now I knew what they were and probably were all along. They were the same string: "fridaynightlights" *Why the HELL wasn't that in my word-lists?* I told him the changes were made after hitting the keys of my keyboard with my phone close to it and told him to call "us" back tomorrow and tell "us" that *he* gave *us* this information. This decision was to just rub the hack into the ISP's disgusting corporate face of course.

I started drinking the last of the rum I had in the fridge and began hacking. Lately, I was drinking more than usual. I was starting to think about alcohol while at work. I guess I was developing a problem. This was weird because, I stopped drinking after my attempt at going through college and haven't cared for it for almost a decade now. Anyways, I was already in the network and in the router as well after spoofing my MAC Address to "69:FE:ED:FA:CE:69" I saw that logging was enabled and disabled it deleting all of the logs. I then checked the two Windows machines for file sharing and scanned their ports. One was actually running an SQL server. *What the hell? A student maybe?* Then I tested a few remote exploits from Metasploit and gained administrative access to that machine alone. I passed the hash to the other machine in hopes that the administrative passwords were the same and, sure enough, they were. In the router I added some port forwarding rules to ensure remote access to these machines when the wireless security settings would change. *Because I am sure they will after tonight.* I backdoored both systems and with the ports aligned, I tested it via my 3g connection. I then changed the wallpaper of the machines to the image I took with my phone after removing all exif data and adding the word "LOL" and a big red arrow pointing at the police car. I started another MiTM attack and ran Wireshark. I saw traffic and then forwarded it all to my machine again with a new message that was just a large Guy Fawkes mask a message below it that said:

"<h1>YOU FUCKING FAIL AT LIFE. THANKS FOR THE FREE INTERNET, I AM GOING TO **DESTROY** YOUR ROUTER IN ONE HOUR FROM NOW. KTXH, PGHFAGS.
ANONYMOUS.</h1>"

I imagine this making news one day and laughed while struggling to restrain myself from telling my friends about it. After only about 10 minutes, their wireless router turned off for about another 10 more minutes. By the time it came back on, I was done writing a simple Perl script that checked to see if they were connected and ran Aireplay-ng to disassociate them from the router for an infinite amount of time. This attacked both wireless devices they had and was completely successful from the output. I noticed them turning the router off and on throughout the night and then it was finally off until morning.

I didn't let up after that. My script ran for days and they had absolutely no access to the internet from this router. When they got a new router, I simply changed the ESSID and BSSID in the Perl script and started it up again. I guess Verizon sent them a new router in hopes that they can again access service. After that a Verizon van was in front of their house the next day. Still, they had nothing. I gave it a few more days before turning off the script and started leeching from a different router that had far less issues.

Ch☠pter 7 - Vultures and Commission

The mall where I worked was a product of a sick and dying economy. The cellular company I worked for had no contracts for their service. In fact, the prepaid service didn't even require the customer to have a valid identification card. I was activating phones for people that claimed their names were the same as famous hip-hop artists. *One can only imagine what the people were like that I had to deal with on a daily basis.*

As with any mall, ours was cluttered with *"authorized"* cellphone providers that were eager to compete with each other, often in evil ways. They were all contract services that probably offered higher commissions considering the lengths the employees went to trying to look like assholes. They hated me. They hated the service that I sold because it was so popular in the area. Customers seemed to swarm my kiosk on busy days. One of them, SuperAdvanced Wireless, would actually send its employees over to my kiosk to talk them into buying from theirs! *The fucking nerve.* They would interrupt a sale I had going with a customer to tell them they could get a handset for free if they just signed a contract.

These people were vultures feeding off of the undecided, under prepared customer. These kiosks would lie to people about hidden fees, take advantage of the elderly, yell out to people walking past the kiosks and even taunt them if they were ignored. It was all very childish and obviously desperate. When I would walk past them to use the restroom, or simply come and go from the mall, they would make faces and laugh at me. I would hear them say things like *"faggot"* and *"freak."* *Who says something like that about someone else they don't even know? Oh yeah, I did. On 4chan.*

There was a limit to my kindness and ability to shrug the shit off from my shoulders after being in the hellish place for eight hours. I was getting mad, bro. One day one of their employees called my store and asked me for customer information. Now, this I would need identification for. That was a security policy in place by the company, not me. In fact, I never gave any account information over the phone to anyone for any reason, no matter who they were. It was a huge security risk! I mean, we used a cordless phone for fucks sake. There are two security vulnerabilities right there to eaves drop from! I didn't care about the guy, I told him too. I told him twice about our policy and just hung up on him.

About one minute later a SuperAdvanced employee came running over to my kiosk holding his pants up and yelling the whole way over. I looked at his kiosk behind him and saw his coworkers just standing there watching him. So, I picked up the phone and dialed the number for mall security which I actually had memorized by then. They didn't show up until after the mess, so after a few minutes, I told him to bring the customer over to my kiosk and I would give her the information they needed. "No, she's not here! It's my girlfriend you dickhead!" He said. This statement silently overflowed the buffer I kept for tolerance of anyone. I made two fists and told him to get away from me. I even saw a woman walking through the mall looking at the scene and snickering at me. Then the manager of the store came over and told me to give his employee the information and called me a "moron." *The fucking manager of a business did this!* "Fuck off," I said as I picked up the phone again for security as they walked away giving me the middle finger calling me a "fucking baby."

The next day, I tried to convince my girlfriend that we needed to purchase two hand held cellphone jammers. Fail. I bought them anyways from money I borrowed from my mother. I went into the As Seen on TV store in the mall and purchased two remote controlled wall outlet plugs. The jamming equipment was coming from the U.K. and took about a week for me to receive them. During this period, I attacked their network using their wireless access point that both of their kiosks shared. Their access point was protected by WPA, so early one morning, I set up my 802.11 protocol analyzer on the access points channel and started capturing packets. When the stores finally opened, I had two handshakes from their remote machines connecting to the access point. My Linux server at home was completely filled with giant sized word lists at this point and I had modified my Perl script that manipulated strings, or words, into not saving a file. The word lists were specifically for WPA offline brute-force attacks. This meant that every line has a different case version, and they are between eight and sixty three characters in length. With the Perl script now modifying a file, I could manipulate gigabytes worth of data without ever having to save anything on the hard disk. I could just pipe the output directly to Aircrack-ng. The next step, was to strip the packet capture file of everything besides the WPA handshakes making it significantly smaller. All beacons and extra, unnecessary data packets were gone using a simple Wireshark filter. I started this up on my server after uploading the handshake file to it.

During the last few days I started using the back corridors more to get to the restrooms. This helped me avoid seeing the other kiosks and I also learned something new. One of the walls in the corridor was lined with four foot tall TNI, or telephone network interface, boxes! *Perfect!*

The next day, my server had found the WPA pass-phrase as

"Racecar06."[21] I had the day off, but I went into work anyways. I had a different job to do. When I got there, I told Sharon, my employee, that I was just there to do some extra work for the store owner. I wasted no time whatsoever attacking their machines. My fingers were programmed to do this as if they had a brain of their own. After scanning for network shares, I found a few that were not password protected and leeched every file they had to offer. A few of the documents I found were from the actual carriers they dealt with. These were documents for new employees which included login names and passwords, but I couldn't find any URLs in them. I found directories full of images the employees took of each other, presumably from cellphones. I instantly thought of all the evil things I could do with these! I also found directories full of mp3's, which too, were presumably for their customers. *Hrmm, copyright infringement too?*

I felt so enraged, but at the same time, I knew what to do. I channeled my anger into productivity and began digging deeper. My accuracy was now razor sharp. I started deleting everything from the shares and began a man in the middle attack on one of the hosts using the Dsniff Suite and Fragrouter. After poking my head up out of the kiosk, I saw one of their employees was at her computer and had a customer. No traffic was coming from the machine I chose to attack, so I let go and attacked another. I did this until I found the one sending and receiving HTTP traffic. I got the IP from a reverse DNS lookup since I didn't recognize the URL and found that it belonged to NEXTEL. Bingo. I now had the URL, username and password for the Nextel login site for activating phones all thanks to an unprotected Windows share. Once I had this, I decided to have fun with her. All of her HTTP requests would now be directed to a website known for, well... goat sex.

I saw a few requests come in and I laid my jacket over my laptop on the floor. Then I stood up and looked around. I saw the horror on the girls face. She then laughed as if she was hiding fear. Her customer

---

[21] Seriously?

started yelling and bent over to look at her computer. I plopped back down onto the floor and started up the AutoPWN script within my msfconsole from Metasploit. This is a script that shot all known vulnerabilities at a target after port scanning it for services. It was a sure fire way to test the latest exploits in Metasploit with great speed. I used it only while multitasking because it was a noisy scan and exploitation method. I knew these idiots didn't have an IDS or any kind of security whatsoever on their machines.

Around this time I was a huge fan of SpoofCard, a service that allowed you to spoof your phone number for the price of only the talk time you used. I used it many times during hacking and when it was really useful. After letting the AutoPWN script fly, I spoofed my phone number to 412-000-000 and called the mall's central guest services desk. I changed my voice to a gruff older man's with a heavy Pittsburgh accent, since most of the clerks knew me by then, and told the clerk that I was extremely irate at the sight of the goat sex on the SuperAdvanced employees computer. I demanded that they took action and threatened to sue the mall over it. She said she would dispatch mall security immediately and asked for my name. I slammed the phone down on the desk and leaned over to see the central desk. I smiled and saw the clerk run over to a nearby security guard who was flirting with a girl that was leaning against a large stone pillar.

I plopped back down and saw shell sessions listed in the mscfconsole on her computer. I opened a second terminal with CTRL+D and ran Figlet with the string "PWNT." I copied the generated ASCII art and connected to the first session shell. I started the "edit" program in the DOS prompt and laid in the figlet text. I was surprised that it didn't get mangled in formatting! I saved the document and opened it with Notepad.exe which popped up on her screen. I then started "C:\Program Files\Internet Explorer\iexplorer.exe" several hundred times, pointing it at the goat sex website, just as the security guards showed up at her kiosk.

I was smiling so hard now, my cheeks were stiff. This was a huge mess for them. The security guards made her close her laptop and call their manager to come into the store. I could tell even from the distance that she was embarrassed. This meant no phone sales until he arrived. My next attack was more fatal. That same night I called my girlfriend and told her I would be very late with Ethermine and to not wait up for me. She told me I was "regressing" when I was with him. She knew I was doing something wrong. I was holding the cellphone jammers in my hands when I said "Don't worry, I'm just trying to make my life less stressful!"

I had no plans with Ethermine. I sent him a text that said I was going to be with him if she were to call or ask. I laid down in the kiosk on the floor when the mall closed. I usually did all of my hacking and prank playing alone. The last time I tried with my brother, the police almost threw us behind bars, so do you blame me? I knew that the back doors had no alarms and they had large bar-like push handles that would let me exit easily after the mall closed.

After a few hours of watching YouTube videos from the previous E3 conference, I stood up and stretched my legs. The place was an absolutely abandoned. It was so peaceful to see, actually. Usually, the place was filled with zombie-like senior citizens, screaming babies and thugs, people yelling into their cellphones, and loud music pouring out of every clothing store. I felt absolute peace for about five seconds. The Christmas decorations were lit up and no one was there to see them, but me. Then I thought about it all and how I needed a new job. To get out of there for good, and alive, would be a miracle. Things were really looking bleak for my future as a customer service representative and manager of a cellphone kiosk, unfortunately.

After walking back into the long corridors, I looked around for any sign of lingering people. Nothing. The place was an absolute post-apocalyptic ghost town. I had pulled the doors off of two of the large TNI boxes before realizing they pretty much were in order as far as physical location and I was able to pinpoint the box for

SuperAdvanced. I planted another cordless beige box into their TNI and wired it right onto their pair. I lifted the giant lid back onto the TNI box and walked back to my kiosk. When I got back I opened my backpack and unscrewed both of the cellphone jammers. After locating the power cables in the units I extended them with pieces of scrap wire to the outsides of the case. I wired an "As seen on TV" remote on off switch into each unit and used black tape to secure the whole thing together. It took me about three minutes to modify the units. Then I planted them in, well, plant pots. One in near each of their kiosks. The plants were against pillars and, as luck would have it, both right next to wall outlets! This allowed me to turn them on remotely at will, jamming up all cellular signals around the complete radius of both stores.

Each day after that I had off, I would call in and ask one of my employees if the manager was there or not. I knew I couldn't call them directly, as they would lie to me, even if I acted like an irate customer. They were complete slime balls. Finally, I had a day off when he was working and I went in with my backpack. I walked into the back of the corridors and flipped on my cordless beige box base. Then, I found a nice seat on a bench in a remote corner of the mall and placed down my bag, soft drink, and flipped on the cordless beige box handset. After a few minutes, it blinked. "My first customer of the day!" I yelled out loud, in a very arrogant manner. "Hello, this is Super Asshole Wireless, how can I screw you over today?" I heard a mans voice on the other end say "Hello?" and I replied instantly with "I think your Mother might know the answer," while keeping a perfectly straight face. Then I hung up on the guy before he could answer.

Another call came through immediately after and I thought it was the same person as before. It was. I answered with "What the fuck do you want?" and he mentioned something about coming up to the store to "beat the shit" out of me. I told him I was the manager and gave him the manager's name.

The next call through and I answered with "Whaddup yo!?" It was the girl at the other kiosk calling. She started talking to me assuming I was one of their employees! Right in the middle of her landing a huge story on me and asking me if I was going to the employee party that Friday, I told her to hold on. I flung open my laptop from my backpack and ran AutoPWN on the same system she was on before. This time, I got a VNC session to her computer and I saw their printer, so I configured it to my machine so I could print to it. I got her back on the phone and said "There I fixed it bitch!" and hung up on her.

I ignored all of the calls that came in for a few minutes, as I started as many processes on her machine as I could. I started the webcam in the laptop and noticed that no one was even looking at the machine. I saw someone on the phone, so I listened in and heard them talking about the shit I was doing to them. It was sad, really. They were clueless. The girl was trying to tell the other guy about what was going on and he just responded by telling her she was smoking her parents crack pipe. What the hell kind of coworker does something like that? I was so mad, that I attacked his machine too and spawned another VNC session. All of the XP machines were so outdated. I started the webcam software and saw his fat face looking directly at me, as if he could see me. I laughed and started to print screen shots of his face to the printer. He was trying to move the trackpad but couldn't keep up with me.

I was filled with joy to do this for some reason. This really wasn't like me so one could imagine how pissed off I was at them. I spoofed my phone number to an 800 number and called the downstairs kiosk. I laid a bullshit story on the girl working about all of the "events" that were taking place and that I worked for "corporate." She completely confided in me because of my faked phone number. That's all it took. She then gave me the manager's cellphone number and told me I should call him. *She* gave *me* the idea. Under the same exact pretenses, I called his cellphone. When he answered I told him I was from corporate and that he had really screwed up. I told him I was receiving complaints from the mall manager about his customers and just then I printed the fat guys face onto his printer multiple times. He was in disbelief but trying to be polite and calm. He told me that he had just showed up to the store and I told him he lied and was there all morning, because he really was. I saw him. He gave me a story about how he must have a virus on his computer and I told him again that he was lying. I asked him who he "screwed over," and he said "no one." "Well, someone is awfully mad at you," I replied. I told him I was going to disconnect his company cellphone service and that he was terminated from the company. I told him I would send mall security to have him escorted from the building and that he should never return to the premises again without calling corporate first.

After hanging up, I did all of those things. I jammed up his cellphone and called the central mall office from their phone number asking them to come up to the kiosks to check out what was going on. *Heh, I called security on myself.* When he hung up the phone, he was holding a bunch of printouts of the fat guys face and threw them at him yelling "What the fuck are you doing!?" I started walking in the direction of his kiosk to see with my own eyes and walked right passed holding my laptop. I heard the guy and a girl saying that their phones were "turned off" too. I saw him fling his cellphone onto the desk when he realized it was not working. When he noticed security guards coming to the kiosk, he yelled something at them and left walking out of the building assuming they were coming to escort him. I removed the cordless beige box from their TNI but left the jammers in place and went home.

The next day, I noticed he was back in the kiosk. I guess he figured out he wasn't fired after all. Each time their company would try to sell a phone for the next few days after that, I made sure the phones didn't work with the jamming equipment. I watched as the frustrated employees removed the batteries of the phones, rebooted them, and even tried more of them opening up new boxes. One day, I noticed that they didn't open up for business and they had blankets draped over their store. That night, I removed the jamming equipment, removed my prints from them and threw them into the public trash cans outside. He should never have existed, let alone fucked with me.

Ch☠pter **8** - The Sniffer Box

IRC is really an amazing thing. Over the years, I have met many inspiring people. I've joined in on projects, given technical support, and received a lot of help too. I really don't know where my life would have gone without it to be honest. With so many new friendships all the time, I was led into some great things.

Once, my friends on the channel #lunatics decided to have a competition. They were trying to see who would come up with the most abundant list of *active* credentials for internet accounts. Usually I never took part in them, because most of them were skilled with remotely rooting web servers, local and remote file inclusion attacks, and SQL injection. This meant when a database was actually scored, it landed them a few thousand accounts. But, if you really think about it, only about 50% of these hacked databases stored passwords in plain text. If one of them decided to use a password cracking machine, or set of machines, he would likely run out of time before the deadline.

I am not sure why, but this time I decided I would join in on it. We promised not to submit anything that we did not hack. This meant that we couldn't just browse PasteBin.com or somewhere for hacked accounts, we actually had to go out and do it. The prize would be the sum of all of our contributed money. I told them the main method I would be using is wireless sniffing to obtain my password list. This only made them laugh and tell me I couldn't do it.

A few months prior to this night, I was exploring a demolished building. It was a large family restaurant that went out of business. I guess the insurance company decided to have the building demolished to rebuild it. While I was exploring the rubble, I found a large VeriZon Fios box. It was about two feet high, a foot across, and 6 inches or so deep. It looked like it had a small car battery in it. I ripped everything out of it and for some reason, I decided to swipe it from the site.

After thinking about how I was going to pull this hack off, I thought about using another router repeater. Then, I just wondered what it would be like to simply sniff packets all day long, from any location. *Sitting there with my laptop would be so annoying and I would end up going home after an hour.* I don't like sitting in public for extended periods of time really. If there were some way I could just leave my laptop there and write scripts to do all of the work for me that would be great. In fact, that *is* great. *That's what I will do.*

My first thought was to hide the laptop on the roof. But, if something were to happen to it, or if someone found it, I would lose everything including the hardware. Then, I thought about the Fios box I found from the demo site that was laying on the table in my basement. I could disguise the laptop as actual telco equipment!

In the basement, I put the Fios box onto my old makeshift work bench and opened it up fully. There was just enough room for my old 7" ASUS EeePC! After drilling a few holes for an external dipole antenna, I used a few pieces of wood to create a base to nest the netbook into. After, I did the same for the power supply. I added a twenty foot black extension cable to the power cable and let it fall out of the bottom of the Fios box. Making sure that the edge of the machine was against the wall of the box, I used a Sharpie marker to mark exactly where the USB port was. Next, I drilled a bigger hole the size of a quarter into the marking. I now had direct access to the USB port from the outer left side of the box. I cut a square from a black garbage bag and used super glue and duct tape to cover the USB hole on the inside of the box.

This is when I got the idea to add my phone into the box. It was an Android phone running CyanogenMod and I had USB tethering capabilities. This way I could use the WiFi radio in the laptop as a fake access point and actually offer some slow internet service while using SSLStrip to get usernames and passwords in clear text. I knew it was kind of dangerous to leave this device outside with my actual phone that was linked to me in in the box, but I figured that if someone found the box and came after me I would deny it and say someone stole my phone. I need to be cautious of security cameras.

I plugged the phone into the netbook and tested the scripts, which worked perfectly. Then, using a razor knife, I cut a one millimeter high slit into the garbage bag square. This would prevent snow or rain from getting directly into the netbook in case of a storm. I used small washers and nuts to secure my ALFA external USB radio to the inside of the case close to the top were I made the hole for the antenna. I also put a large bolt and nut into case of the box so that the bolt stuck directly out of the back of the box closer to the top. This way, I could use it to hang the box on a wall. Next I wired it all up and closed it. It looked very normal to the unsuspecting, I imagined.

Now the box would use the internal Atheros based card to sniff on all channels for nearby AP data and the external WiFi radio would host a fake AP for victims to connect to and the 3g Phone would be tethered to route all traffic to the internet after being stripped of SSL. What a beautiful creation! Thankfully, I had an unlimited data plan with my cellular carrier!

Back in my room, I had the netbook on my desk and started coding some scripts that would watch the PCI bus for changes. The netbook had a tiny version of Linux on it that didn't even have a GUI. I added Perl and all of the Perl modules needed for the Netgh0st application I wrote to scan for resources and enumeration of the local network appliances. I modified it to actually copy data from the Windows network shares this time and set the application to automatically run after associating with the network. Once the OS saw a new USB storage device it would attempt to mount it, copy the latest packet capture files from Airodump-ng, unmount the drive, and then delete the packet capture files, restarting Airodump-ng. I only had to test it out a few times, as it was very easy to code. I had to put in a safety subroutine that made sure the file was successfully copied to the USB drive before unmounting it and removing it from the hard disk. If it detected a failure, it would simply do it again. After a few tests, it never failed. Now I just needed to write the start-up script that would automatically put the ALFA radio into monitor mode and start the base station with IP forwarding, SSLStrip and packet capturing. This is easy, but what ESSID should I use? "Free Internet" would do, I'm sure. Besides that, I was pretty much ready to plant my new device. I needed to find a heavily populated public access point with an external wall outlet. I found one in the first spot I looked. It was a heavily populated coffee shop that offered free WiFi. *Bingo*.

The next morning, around 3AM or so, I rode my bike up to the coffee shop with the Fios box, and a few other things, in a camping bag on my back. When I got there, it was pitch black. No street lights made their way into the outside sitting area of the coffee shop's nook that overlooked the whole shopping plaza. I leaned my bike against the wall and looked around in all directions. Crouching down I flipped the bag over my shoulder and pulled out the huge Fios box laying it face down. Then, I pulled out a tub of plaster, a putty knife, a drill with a concrete drill bit, and a tube of caulking that the previous owner of my house left in my basement.

I quickly plugged the drill into the wall and made a hole in the mortar between bricks about three feet directly above where the power outlet was. I learned how to drill though brick from a Comcast technician that drilled through my townhouse to run cables a few years before. I completely caked the backside of the Fios box with plaster all around where the bolt stuck out of it. Then, I lifted it up pressing it against the wall, letting the bolt slide directly into the hole I made. Then I thought to myself that the plaster probably wasn't needed. The bolt was really solid and would probably support the weight of the box on its own. I pulled open the door and turned on the computer after pulling the LCD completely upwards. I noticed that it started to snow lightly and the breeze made me feel rushed. I watched it boot up and I closed over the LCD, leaving it open about one and a half inches to let the heat come out of it. Before closing over the lid of the Fios box, I let just enough cable out of the bottom to plug the netbook on the wall below.

Twice the next day, around 1pm and 6pm, I put on a Verizon technician jacket I bought from Ebay.com a few years before and went out to the box. I put the USB drive into the side and watched as it blinked rapidly. This meant that data was being transferred to it from my scripts. While the transfer was in progress I would check my text messages on the phone I left there all day. Once the transfer was completed, the blinking would turn into a long pulse and I would know to remove the USB drive.

After analyzing the data, I had some great stuff, but not a lot. I had active cookies, email passwords, social networking passwords, and a few other non SSL, or encrypted passwords. All of these worked. The cookies allowed me to login to the accounts that were encrypted with SSL, like Gmail.com and SSL enabled social networking sites. I knew I had to find a bigger target. So, again, around 2am I rode up to the coffee shop and removed the Sniffer Box from the wall stuffing it into my camping bag on my back after scraping off the dried up plaster that was just crumbing away. I rode over to the local library and repeated the process of putting the device on the wall. This time, the wall outlet and I were exposed to the street. So, each time a car drove past, I would have to drop everything and lay down next to the wall by the bushes to not be seen. Usually, this late at night, there wasn't much traffic to worry about. After securing it to the wall and making sure the netbook was running, I went back home for the night.

Life was so weird being away from my phone and communication to my IRL friends. This time I only returned once to retrieve the data before removing the box later that night. This was a huge payload. I guess there was a shared wireless network between the library and a local high school, or maybe the access point was tied directly into the high school. My Netgh0st scans returned a ton of shared data, about 4GB worth. I had user names and passwords to internal web applications, email, and all of the other normal internet resources people use when on a wireless network as well. My list was now pretty impressive for only using a wireless attacking point. While browsing over the data in Wireshark, I looked over at the Sniffer Box on the floor leaning against the wall. *Man, that thing is incredible! No one would ever suspect a thing!*

That night, I was on my IRC channel watching my friends brag about how many logins they had, which were much more than mine. I got a private message from a girl in the channel, Grrly, and began talking to her about the others. She was proud of the amount of logins she had from a simple cross site script vulnerability. Grrly was probably the only one in the channel I was beating, but didn't have the heart to tell her. There were only a few days left and I just had to pull higher numbers. I decided to add support for WPA2 Enterprise Phishing into the netbook. This would host a local Apache server that only had one page. The page was generated dynamically by checking the users browser agent and it was a simple, fake, "no connection" page. It would display the correct error for the browser, and after about two or three seconds would display a fake Windows, or OSX, wireless login window. I even went as far as allowing the user to hit the "X" button and making it return. You could even drag the window around just as if it were from the actual window manager using jquery. The window was basically a screenshot of the actual window that would pop up when you were asked for the WiFi password by the operating system. In our case, we asked for WPA2 user name, password, and optional domain name. Next, I installed a bigger antenna into the Sniffer box, which passively boosted its transmit power and range dramatically.

Once tested and ready, I took my Sniffer Box to a university in my city. I planted it late at night on the side of a building were students would congregate to study, or just browse the web and changed its ESSID to one commonly used on campus. Needless to say, I gained most of my WiFi data up to this point from this score. About every hour, or so, I had at least 100 EAPOL passwords and more. The radio was also sniffing for everything on that channel, which caught a lot of unencrypted traffic from access points around it. I made a few trips over to the building with my USB drive and ended up just booking the next night at a hotel close by. I spent the next two days in front of my computer screen compiling a huge list of user names and passwords before heading home.

Now, I had a few holes around the city to plant my Sniffer Box whenever I wanted to, but the contest was almost over. I found some personal info on Grrly starting with an old Myspace.com page she accidentally left around before becoming a hacker. I used this information as a means to land her house address, family member's names, and even a few phone numbers. I decided to prank call her so I spoofed my phone number to "1010101010" and called her. A man answered the phone and sounded like he had been drinking. I could hear her in the background trying to wrestle the phone from him and when she got on the line, I acted like the Pittsburgh Police looking for a man called "Seadog." She knew right away it was me. We laughed about it and I rubbed it in her face that I had close to a thousand logins from raiding the wireless empire of my city. She couldn't believe it. Her XSS attack was caught and fixed just after she told me about it, so she blamed me to ratting her out and still didn't have much. After trying to talk to her about her drunken father, she just seemed too depressed. I felt really bad for her. I wanted to win this just to give her the cash.

That night, I modified the code for Airodump-ng to spit out all of the AP channels into a file that had the strongest signal and I added a third WiFi radio to the Sniffing Box. Now there were two antennas sticking out of the top of the box. This would now channel hop to find the strongest signals, dump them to a file, then Perl would read the file and hop in 10 minute intervals between those channels only. This way, I didn't have to sit there and find them myself. I knew this was the last and final day and that even if I didn't win, I did a damn good job so far. So, I decided to add an actual external USB hard disk into the box itself. This time, I had Ethermine drive me down to the city to plant the box. I told him all about the box and what I was doing. He thought the story about the girl on IRC was really sad and offered to help. I put it right in the middle of my city around 4am. It was now getting pretty heavy, but I had no problems at all planting it behind two buildings. We took off to a state park and fished in Lake Arthur for the rest of the day. As we talked he recommended that I let the contest go. Let her win. If I gave her my logins, she would surely win and I would feel okay about it. Besides, I didn't really need the cash at all, so I agreed.

When we got back to the city it was only about 6pm and I just wanted to see if the box was capturing data okay. I plugged in a USB thumb drive to the port on the side and waited as it blinked. It took longer than normal, so I thought that it must have captured more data than I had expected. After grabbing my cellphone out of the box checking my messages, I flicked a cigarette on the ground and a man walked around the corner of the alley right behind me. I carelessly left my VeriZon jacket in the car, so I just flung open my phone and called Ethermine to swing around and come get me. I looked at the man and he was looking directly back at me walking quickly. I glanced at the USB drive and the damn thing was still blinking! When he got closer I noticed he was a rent-a-cop. Shit.

"Hey buddy, wait up!" he yelled as I began to walk away. I turned and kept pace while saying "Yeah, what do you want?" "Just cah-mere! I just want to ask you something abaht this box, I saw you here earlier.

What the hell you doing to their service?! I'm calling the police right now! They are on their way!" He yelled. I cringed at his thick Pittsburgh accent. I hated that sound. He was a big arrogant mouth-breathing Stillers fan. Just then Ethermine drove up behind him quickly and laid on his horn to scare the guy. I left my phone open so Ethermine was listening to the whole thing. The cop spun around to him and pulled up the badge hanging around his neck yelling "Whoa! Slow dahn mahr fahker!"

I took the opportunity to run as fast as I could. I ran completely around the building and stealthily came back up behind Ethermine's car. I leaned against a nearby dumpster. I noticed Ethermine got out of his car and was talking to the cop acting really stupid and apologetic. This always worked. When he drove off and the cop rounded the bend I ran up to the Sniffer Box and swiped the USB drive from it and ran back the opposite direction. Ethermine texted me and said the cop called in a suspicious looking man with a VeriZon hat on and a red shirt with black pants that had fled the scene. *Shit, shit, shit. Wait. A VeriZon hat? I am wearing my Phonelosers of America hat! Heh.* I stopped at a dumpster and took off the hat. I looked at it and figured I could just buy another one. I flung it into the dumpster beside me and took off my pants. Standing there in my underwear I took out a folding knife I had in my pocket from fishing and cut them into shorts. Then, I took off my outer shirt and flung all of the fabric and clothes into the dumpster. I heard police sirens and my heart started to race as I thought about the worst. I left the alley wearing only an undershirt, make-shift shorts, socks and shoes. *God damn, its cold outside.* I ducked into a bus stop and thought about having Ethermine pick me up there. It was too risky. If the cop thought we were partners he would be looking out for his car. I decided to leave the city and take whatever bus came to that stop. Ethermine text me again a message about how nothing on his police scanner said anything about the Sniffer Box. This was good, they thought it was real and left it there. *Heh.*

I used my main Android phone with Google Maps to find out where the bus was actually taking me and called Ethermine to get me. The longer I was on the bus, the better it was, as it was very cold now in the city at night. I worked on the new packet capture file until 1pm the next day. It was just simply too much. I had so many user names and passwords, that I was completely shocked. I had pulled off one of the biggest hacks of my small hacking career and all I exploited was the fact that WiFi RF was a shared medium of communication! *Without strong encryption, or with strong encryption, our data is transmitted everywhere. Identities, passwords, data, systems, and services all open up the possibilities for a black hat hacker. All I had to do was "listen."*

This is ridiculous. A few hours after, around 3pm, I went back down to the city. I opened the box, leaving it on the wall and pulled out the computer and the hard drive. I stuffed the power supply into my pocket and walked away quietly. No one noticed me this time, I hoped. I got the drive mounted and I was again, astonished by the huge amount of usable data I had. The amount of cookies was phenomenal. I was swimming in it all when the time came to tally up with the others on IRC.

Each of us told our totals and I had the second largest amount. Grrly had the fourth largest amount. No one believed that I had so many, so I told them I didn't and that I lied. *I lied about lying.* I told them that I forfeited. No one even believed that, and begged me for my logins. *Too late.* I sent my list to Grrly and she added it to hers and she ended up winning the competition. She was so excited. I felt really good about the whole thing too. She told me later that she used the cash for school supplies.

The weekend passed and I was finally on my way back to work, walking through the city streets. I walked through the alley where the Sniffer Box was planted on the wall and tore it off. I pulled the black extension cord completely out of the bottom and let it drop to the ground. Then I removed the ALFA radios and antennas, stuffing them into my pockets. *Did they really think this was a piece of VeriZon equipment? I should have been caught a long time ago. Heh.* I dropped it on the ground after noticing a Bell can in the same alley. I put two of my fingers into two adjacent holes straddling the lid and lifted it sweeping the box down into the hole with my foot saying "Here, take yer shit back." I watched it land on pipes and cables about twelve feet below. I let the can lid slide down and I kicked it closed with my foot. *Fuck them.*

From this day forward, I was changed again. I was so fascinated by wireless technologies that I decided to focus all of my hacking power on it. I began reading RF engineering books and taking online practice tests. I started learning more about networking, and all of the accompanying mathematics. It was all just too juicy to leave alone. It was the strongest addiction I had come across up until that point in my life.

Ch☠pter 9 - Post Mortem

Wednesday. Another boring day in the basement. It's been 7 months since I quit that job. I haven't put a lot of thought into it since, but I have begun to consider that I might actually be able to get some revenge for the trouble I had with those idiots. So, after a few hours of contemplating, I began planning, and realized just how easy it would be. Good, some cold pizza still in the fridge. I'm hungry.

Two hours later, I had my backpack, laptop, and everything else I needed and was on my way to the target. I arrived at 6am the sun was just about to rise. I climbed the ladder at the back of the building. I was finally on the rooftop with my equipment, laptop check, 250 watt collapsible solar unit unfolded, battery and inverter, check. Now, that I have power. It's time to get to work.

So here I am, on the rooftop, directly above my target victim. With power, a laptop, a *Mikrotik* access point and a vendetta. I begin by setting reconnaissance. Sniffing out nearby open access points, I've got to get a link up to my more powerful computers hosted elsewhere.

I'm going to need some raw power to crunch some of these encryption keys. Starbucks, that'll work. I setup a client, and now I have internet. Next, I setup a fake access point, spoofing their ESSID. I will trick their wireless clients into connecting to my rogue access point, submitting a WPA key into a false login. I will also be setting up a guest wireless virtual access point with my *Mikrotik* and bridging the internet connection I just secured in case anything, or anyone interesting near of the target area connects to my router, I will have their data as well.

Meanwhile, my fake AP is setup, ready to capture the WPA key. Next, I begin my frontal assault against their routers. The goal: to crack their encryption keys manually and gain direct access to their network for packet capture and analysis. I know if I wait long enough I will likely get one of them to submit it at my fake access point, but I really, really want to get into their network now. So, I fire up *Aircrack-NG* and generate some handshakes. It doesn't take long.

I just uploaded them to my remote network, *pyrit* CUDA. It's cracking. I figure a 20GB wordlist outta suffice against these fucking noobs. I wait, reclined against my backpack, pilot sunglasses on, watching the sun rise as my machines do my bidding. Shouldn't be long now. After waiting a little while longer, I sit back up and look down at my screen eagerly anticipating verification of the key, and just then I see it:

KEY FOUND: ImaSecureBoss11

Guess you're not so secure after all, "boss." Now, I have a decision to make. Authenticate to their access point with the key, or I can setup my fake AP, spoof their MAC and ESSID, and use their own security key. I want to make sure I get it all. I want passwords, I want logins, I want privilege escalation, I want everything, and today, I am going to get it. So, I decided to simply authenticate to their network using the WPA2 key I just decrypted. Now, I'm in. I have this motherfucker by the balls and there is no way in Hell I'm letting go. For the wasted time dealing with this moron, the low pay, the denigration, oh yes, there's going to be Hell to pay this day. Just before I could make my next move, the network engineer arrives in his overpriced *Landrover*. I mumble to myself "That's right go inside and drink your stinking coffee you fucking prick." I hated the stink of his coffee breath every time he had to give one of his authoritarian talks. I wanted to vomit from the stink of this man's face. And now vengeance was about to be mine. I was salivating excessively, my mouth literally watering.

I could taste revenge.

I fire up a few tools, *IMSpector Proxy*, for Instant messaging interception, *Wireshark*, and of course *Ettercap-NG*. I've got everything setup and now I wait. As the hours progress and all the employees begin to show up, I look down and check my power system, everything looks good, suns up now, battery is full, solar panels deployed, inverters charging, laptops running good, Damn, I'm hungry again.

6 hours later. I have collected over 3GB of traffic, this outta be plenty. Now I'm going to take this information home with me for the big payoff. Carefully, and methodically, I begin packing up all my gear. I pause, considering my position. I cannot resist. It must be done. But, not from here, I'll do it from the car.

I leave my laptop running, so it doesn't disconnect from their network, keeping the MitM going. I'm in the car now, ready to go. But, one last thing. I load up a custom *Ettercap-NG* filter and load a *Photoshopped* image of my boss in a fag pose. Index to the Return key.

I'm enjoying every second, watching my own finger come down like a slow motion sledge hammer. "Click" it's done, every image , on every website, on every browser on that network will only get that image. I can see them live in the network security system, I can see their reactions OMG lulz! This is priceless.

Fun's over, it's time to go. I casually pull out and head home with the booty.

Chapter 10 - Something's Burning

I wanted some good experience with embedded Linux and decided to find an easily modifiable router online. I found the Linksys WRT160NL from Cisco on Amazon.com and did some simple research on DD-WRT and OpenWRT compatibility. This was an amazing device, which offered an amazing chipset from Atheros, a USB port and a lot more flash memory than the old WRT54g models. Unfortunately, at the time of my purchase, none of the mainstream precompiled embedded router operating systems supported the device fully. I bought it anyways because of the specifications it offered and the low price and tried compiling a new kernel for it on my Debian machine. After a week, it seemed that I just couldn't get it quite right. I eventually caved and began spending more time hacking other things and started using the router as a second access point in our house.

About a year went passed before I decided to give the router a second shot. Now, OpenWRT had more support for the router, but still had some radio issues. I decided to install it anyways because of how easy the process was. Dealing with issues in Linux, really tends to give a person great hands-on experience. I then added a simple kernel modification to support a USB thumb drive as a block device and used it to store larger applications. I spent about an hour trying to get the device up and running before realizing that I had to reseat the USB drive and rerun the mount command! One really amazing thing about OpenWRT is the package manager opkg. It always seems to work great no matter what hardware I am using. They have a lot of recoded precompiled packages listed for each model of router on their website. I altered the configuration files for opkg and added my new USB drive as a storage unit for the applications. I then spent a few hours, going through the packages and dependencies, installing everything I wanted to use. This is now a full-blown wireless hacking weapon. Some of the tools I added were Nmap, Aircrack-ng suite, Ettercap-ng, AircrackPTW, AirPWN, Bash, Dsniff, WGET, and BitchX. I even found a driver for my ALFA WiFi card! This means that if I used a small USB hub I could have storage and radio functionality simultaneously! My next task was to get a fully working copy of Metasploit installed on it. If this was going to be my new Router Repeater, I would need to attack machines directly from its shell. I had to find and install almost every Ruby library package file on the OpenWRT website that I could find. Once done, the router ran Metasploit, almost flawlessly.

After giving the new Router Repeater a lot of attention for software, I did some research online for external batteries. This hack would be so much easier to do than to rely on external power sources, by making the device even more mobile than it already was. I found myself putting a 12VDC, five port USB hub, and a 14dbi panel antenna for my ALFA card all in the same shopping cart online. All of the new hardware took about a week to come in the mail and by that time I was neck deep into another huge hack which involved a government office in the city who decided to share all of their files on a network guarded with a weak WEP key. So, I threw the router, battery, antenna, hub and USB radio into an old plastic milk crate for later use. A few days had passed and one night I was woken up by my girlfriend who was panicking because our house was filled with smoke. I was extremely groggy from the combination of a deep sleep and the lack of oxygen. I ran into my office and saw the ceiling fan lying on the desk and flames were shooting out of the hole in the ceiling above where it used to be. The third floor was on fire and we had animals up there. I opened up the door and ran up the steps, but the smoke and massive amount of heat produced a physical wall that I couldn't get past. There was a second door to the room where the fire had started, where the animals were and my girlfriend pried it open. Thick black smoke poured out like water and the heat was enough to make me fall backwards on the stairs. She ran down stairs to call the police and I knew there was nothing I could do. The fire was just too strong and had been burning for hours inside the floor while we were sleeping.

I once wondered as a kid what things I would try to save from my house being on fire, if I could only grab two things. Those two things in this case were our dogs Igby and Pigeon.

I stood outside in the snow with my pajamas on in the dark holding the collars of two rambunctious large dogs, on a Newfoundland and the other a Great Pyrenees. I watched as firemen poured into my house with axes, propped up the ladder, and extended the firehouse all the way up to my third floor.

By the time it was over, the third floor and everything on it was destroyed. My computer laboratory server room was right below and it too was destroyed. The ceiling was gone and I could see directly up into the third floor. Black soot, wood, carpeting, plaster, and water covered everything. That day, I buried three of our other pets and we had to vacate our home and move into a hotel in the city.

After being inspected, it turned out that the fire started from having old knob and tubing wires in our old home. An event like this adds a huge amount of stress to one's daily life. It took us a long time to clean up from this and I still, to this day, get spooked when I catch a scent of a fireplace or outdoor grill.

I lost everything that I had built for my laboratory. It was now dwindled down to a simple weblog and free software. I spent a lot of my own free time in the hotel coding Android applications for my Android phone and writing tutorials for other weblogs and forums on WiFi hacking. This helped me rekindle some of the spirit I had, but I never fully got it all back. Problems arose with my relationship with my girlfriend and things between us just seemed like they couldn't get any worse and they actually never got much better.

In February of 2010, just days after the fire, a huge snow storm took over Pittsburgh like a huge, white, heavy blanket. It was locally dubbed "Snowpocalypse." Several feet of snow fell as I hid in the hotel room watching television and hacking. Each night, I would get an automated call from the university where I worked telling me to stay home the next day. I didn't listen. I took my gear out to explore the city that was covered in snow. It was amazing. I could walk right in the middle of usually crowded, busy streets and tunnels. I opened up Bell cans that were too visible on any other day or night in the middle of the road. I guess it did kind of live up to the apocalyptic tagline in some aspects. I had free reign over everything that I saw and wanted to explore.

Unfortunately, this just made things even worse with my relationship. I never really understood why my hobbies were disliked by her, when all they did was give me experience and fuel my passion to have a better career. We were quite well off because of all the years I spent pining away in our apartments studying physics and computer science. It is incredibly hard to obtain and maintain a great job in IT without a college degree and I wasn't really good at anything else. I knew that I was too old to get a career in a physics or science position. That would require just far too much effort and many school loans. Plus, I tried college twice since high school and both times my life just seemed to get in the way. Each time I got a new position or moved within my department, I was making a higher salary than before. I was living high in the moment. Most of my closest friends had become more and more distant over time and I actually spent more time with my online friends in IRC channels. Through my interactions with society during the period of my life, I gathered that very few people can find actual beauty in mathematics, science, and IT. Most of the people I talked to hated mathematics, thought that science was okay, or said that they never had the urge to use a computer before. *How is this possible?*

What I was doing was providing thrill, awe, experience and well, money! Yeah, I was profiting from my hacking, but not by extortion. I would hack the living hell out of a company and just walk away with the experience of doing so. It gave me more knowledge and power over the next hack, more to explain in interviews and while teaching my peers, and made me more confident and comfortable in my career. I didn't care about the data, or showing anyone after the fact really. *I just wanted to know. I just wanted the thrill.*

Ch☠pter **11** - The Router Repeater (Part II)

Each day during our stay at the hotel, we would take a ride out of the city and into the suburbs to our partially destroyed house to salvage some of our belongings. The insurance company asked us for all of our clothing to have them dry cleaned and gave us sheets of paper to list all of the items that were destroyed on the third and second floor of our house. We would go through and snap pictures with our phones of the items and spent a lot of time writing those lists making sure everything was on there. One night while at our house, I saw the milk crate with the Router Repeater equipment in it and decided to grab it to play with it at the hotel. Later, when I we got back to the hotel I scanned the air with Airodump-ng and saw a lot of networks and traffic. In the immediate city area, every company had wireless networks. One network of particular interest really stuck out at me as being a great target. I locked onto the channel and MAC address of the AP with Airodump-ng and I couldn't see any significant traffic or get a strong enough signal to attack it from the comfort of the hotel. I plugged the external 12VDC battery into the wall to change it and closed over the laptop lid after shutting down the 802.11 protocol analyzer.

A few days had passed and I was lying on the bed in the hotel room watching TV. I wasn't paying attention though, I was thinking about hacking. *I was getting that warm feeling in my lungs and considering attacking that AP I found a few days ago.* My girlfriend was at work for the evening shift and I decided to get up and do something.

I cut the power cords to the USB hub and Router then used a multi-meter to determine the polarization of the ports. After that, I wired the external battery to power the devices and tested them. It all worked just fine. I called down to the front desk and politely asked for some garbage bags. They said they would bring them up later, but I didn't want to wait. I rushed down to the desk to grab them. When I was in the lobby I noticed that it had started to snow very heavily outside again and thought about how most of my hacking took place when the weather was bad.

When I got back to the room, I worked really fast. I grabbed a roll of digital camouflage duct tape out of my backpack and threw my lock pick set onto the bed next to the crate. Then I taped the hub, battery and router all together like and covered them with a garbage bag. I then lined the inside bottom portion of the crate with the other garbage bag and put the Router Repeater into it. Then I covered the whole thing again with a white towel from the room. I attached the panel antenna to the outside of the crate with a piece of tape and made sure the whole thing was powered on and ready. I used two ALFA adapters, one to connect to the Router Repeater, and the one with the panel antenna to hack other routers. Before running out of the room, I stuffed some socks into my pockets.

I found the stairwell and made it up to the top. A door with a BEST lock on it, and a ladder against the wall that led up to a trap door were the only two ways out. Climbing the ladder and picking the lock at the top while trying to balance wasn't as appealing as simply picking the lock on the door. I pulled out my favorite hook tool and a tension wrench out of the black zipper case. I put the handle of the tension wrench into the barrel of the lock and with slight pressure against the pins and my ear close to the door I pulled it out slowly, counting the pins. Five pins. I flipped the tension wrench around, put it in properly, and used the hook to set the pins a few times before finding the right setting. I like to not look at the lock while doing this, because it always distracts me. I pretend that the hook tool is an extension of my hands to give me full control of what was going on in the tumbler.

After a few minutes, I opened the lock. I turned the tension wrench only slightly so that I don't have to re-pick the lock to lock it back up. I turned it just enough to open the door. I put a sock between the door and threshold where the lock is so that it wouldn't click each time I opened the door. This was stealthy and made sure that I wasn't going to get locked out on the roof. I ran back down to the hotel room and grabbed the milk crate. Stopping for a second, I was distracted by my reflection in the mirror. *That guy looks excited.* I took a deep breath and flew back up the stairs to the door. As I got out onto the roof, it was completely covered in a few inches of snow and still snowing really heavily. I opened up an umbrella and flipped open my netbook. I connected to the Router and followed the signal strength to the target using Airodump-ng and it led me all the way at the opposite end of the building. I crossed over four and six foot ledges onto other rooftops until I found the target. The radio had good signal strength, but I noticed a lot of noise. This was probably due to the huge transmit power and the low receive power of the shitty ALFA adapter. I couldn't get the traffic that I was generating through the walls and roof of the building. I ripped the tape off of the crate and lowered the antenna with its cable down against a window high up on the building. Right now, I was really praying that no one was in the building near that window!

Once again, the signal wasn't good enough to attack the AP, so I propped the umbrella over my laptop and ran back down to the hotel room. I returned with a 15 foot active USB extension cable and removed the ALFA radio from the secured tape on the Router Repeater. I reconnected it to the Router Repeater, secured it all back into the crate under the towel, and lowered the antenna back down to another window. I finally found a strong enough signal to the target AP through the thick walls and floors of the building. Just then I noticed police lights blinking off of the edge of another building below and saw that there had been an accident in the snow. From where I was standing I could plainly see that it was a fender bender between a minivan and the cop car. I knew that he wouldn't see me if I stayed back away from the ledge enough, but I was still nervous. No matter how cold it was, I could still feel a layer of sweat on my back. With everything now secured and a strong return signal from the target AP, I returned back to my hotel room leaving my Router Repeater in place.

I sat in the soft chair behind the desk next to the window and connected back to the Router Repeater. Then, I started scanning with the other radio and finally, after replaying some packets, I caught a WPA2 handshake. Next, I used SCP and brought the .cap file back to my laptop from the Router Repeater and put it onto my Android phone. I then used SCP again from the Android device to put the cap, or packet capture, file on our Amazon EC2 server that we used solely for cracking WPA keys using a brute force method and Pyrit. I ran a script in a screen session that I wrote that would notify me when Pyrit had completed the attack against the cap file and disconnected from the server from my phone. Now I was dead tired for some reason. I honestly thought, while considering the target, that they would have used a WPA key that was very strong and not in my dictionary file and that this is where the hack stops. Lying on the bed, I opened Google Maps, found a pizza shop just two streets over, and ordered food. I dropped the phone down onto the bed and closed my eyes.

I was woken to the sound of banging on the hotel room door. I jumped up and felt my blood pressure high, ringing in my ears, and my pulse was much faster than normal. *I need to find a new hobby!* After creeping to the door and looking through the peephole to see the pizza delivery guy, I waited a few seconds to see if he would look left or right to someone that could have been hiding. *Yeah, hacking makes you paranoid.* The coast was clear.

I opened the door, paid for the food, threw it on the desk next to the computer and logged back into the EC2 with my phone via SSH. To my surprise, the key had been found by Pyrit! I swallowed down some of the food while connecting back to the Router Repeater and to the target AP. Once on the network, I could see a lot of machines. I muted the television that had been on and blasted Evol Intent on my laptop with XMMS. I fired up Ettercap-ng, Nmap, and grabbed as much WAN and LAN information as possible from the network. *This was all automatic now. I had a routine. I'd crash the Pirate Ship into a Network and just loot it for all it was worth.* Next was the, sometimes failed, task of setting up extra route tables in the router so that I can connect to the machines in the network I was about to pillage. It was successful, so I started up msfconsole from Metasploit and started attacking services on the networked machines. A few administrative Meterpreter sessions opened up on one of the machines that had been running an old SMB Windows share and started taking screen shots to see if anyone was at the terminal.

I mounted a share on my laptop from the router as a network share and started storing data on it from the compromised machine. After poking around, I noticed that there was a wireless adapter on the system and I used the netsh commands to scan the inside of the protected building. This brought another hard target to light! I knew that this one was the mother ship of the company. *I need this.* I was betting that the walls were covered in protective film to not let so much of the clear WiFi signal to leak out. But, I was already in thanks to the transmit power of the ALFA adapter. The top of my body was now moving in rhythm with the drum and bass music as my fingers flew over the keys of my Pirate Ship.

The machine I had compromised had no internet access, so I had to do things a bit more complicated. I downloaded a few tools from Nirsoft.com from my Android device and sent them via SCP to the Router and then through Meterpreter to the compromised machine. These tools produced some saved passwords from the system that I stored in my new profile of the company. The netsh command for viewing the wireless network profiles produced, in clear text, the password to the wireless network that I wanted. It was almost double in size compared to the key I had just cracked with Pyrit. It wasn't a word or combination of words, and contained a lot of special characters. *This network must be really special.*

I dropped the connection to the AP and connected to the newly found AP and began the whole process of setting up the route and scanning all over again. This network had many more machines on it. My NetGh0st tool couldn't even determine the manufacturer of a few of them. I used Metasploit to gain access to all of them this time. I had shells on all but one system that looked like a Linux system. After port scanning it, I saw MySQL running and a web server. From the screen shots on the compromised systems, I saw that they were simple Windows XP machines and most of them had special software open to control scientific equipment in what, I now gathered, was the laboratory. I started downloading everything I could from the network shares and drives of the compromised machines. My Profile on this place was getting rather large! I found some saved bookmarks to the Linux machine that ran the database and I then began testing them with SQLmap. The links had GET parameters to familiar column names and, after testing, I was able to get the whole database. It contained plain text usernames and passwords, data from the scientific equipment, and even data from outside sources. I tested the plain text passwords to the SSH server it was running, but failed each time.

I then decided to do a search on the C:\ drives of the compromised machines for PPK files, which would allow me to login to them without even passing the password. Soon, I had a non-root shell on it. It was a RHEL machine. I went directly to the web root after finding it in the Apache2 configuration and tarred all of the files saving back to my Router Repeater and Pirate Ship. As the files were flying back to my ship, I leaned back in my chair and looked at the muted television. I was so deep in thought that I can't recall what was even on it. I used the bathroom and ate more of the cold pizza on the desk while staring out the large hotel window at the falling snow. I knew that the battery of the Router Repeater was about to die, so I jumped back into my chair to see what else I could grab from the laboratory. I uploaded a tarball of local buffer overflow exploits to the RHEL machine and gained root access after testing just two. I dropped into a bash shell from the standard sh and began clearing all logs and activity of my presence. I exited the system and connected back to the first AP. I spawned new shells on the same machine I compromised before and began removing all evidence of my existence again. It was so amazing to me that I did all of this so quickly before the external 12VDC battery died. Once it finally did, I made my way back up to the rooftop of the hotel.

As I made my way through the door and out onto the roof, I noticed that it was snowing so heavily that it covered all of my tracks from being up here before. I saw the crate on the ledge of the last roof covered in snow and made my way over to it. When I think back to the event, I see the snow falling in slow motion. It was so exciting and such a thrill that I felt accomplished and loaded with power. I looked over to the other buildings and I could barely see them through the falling snow. It was so beautiful. It was now on my shoulders and I could feel it on my head. It truly doesn't snow as often as it seems here. I just, for some odd reason, end up hacking when it does. I feel safer as if it obscures my presence.

After a few minutes, I grabbed the router, reeled up the antenna and dropped it back into the crate, and made my way back to the door. I removed the sock from the door jamb and used my tension wrench to lock up the door.

Back down in the hotel room, I sat in the arm chair of the desk looking at my blinking cursor. I typed ls –l and saw my profile on the laboratory. My clothes were wet and I felt cold. My girlfriend was back at the hotel now and in the shower. My music was off and the television was now unmuted. It was playing the song "Run" from Collective Soul. I sighed before having a flashback to middle school. I was sitting in the principal's office with him and my Algebra teacher. I was there for being disruptive and drawing obscene pictures on his chalkboard. I always liked math. In fact, I love it more now than I did while in school. I'm not good at it, but I really love it. Unfortunately for my future, I liked making people laugh and getting attention even more back then. I had trouble being accepted as a runt in a poor community. The Algebra teacher told me and the principal that I was really smart, but I would most likely grow up to use my intelligence to the wrong reasons. He said that I needed guidance to become more positive. Well, I never got it. *Look at me now, using skill to break the law and with no great excuse except for the thrill of it all.*

I eventutally came back to, and after spending time rummaging through the files, *I found gold*. From the scientific laboratory data, I found documents, schematics, source code, and a special OS image *specifically* designed for a very common router used here in the North Eastern US. This special image was targeted at accommodating for the manufacturer's tendency to use several chipset manufacturers and additional ports per router revision of the same models. *A universal image that could be ported from router to router without driver problems? This could come in handy one day!* I also noticed from the documents about the image, that the radio power could be controlled in a strange manner, the kernel was optimized for low memory usage and there was added support for various file-system types. *If they went through all of the trouble of securing this place, then why did they leave the image in a shared directory?* I saved all of it for later use and closed over the lid of the laptop.

The WiFirus

Ch☠pter 12 - WiFirus

After being in the hotel for a month, our insurance company found us an apartment to stay in that would accommodate us and our dogs until the contractors completed the repairs. This took roughly another nine months. Being out of the hotel and city was slightly comforting, and the suburbs offered a lot of resources to practice my WiFu skills. During our stay in the temporary apartment, I was offered another position at my job as an application specialist and a huge pay raise. Finally, no more break-fix work for me. This would change everything. All of my programming and hacking truly paid off. I know these aren't huge successes, but I cherish each one and it never failed. After my router repeater encounter with the scientific laboratory, I found it a huge coincidence that the university offered a similar project to me. This project, along with a lot of creativity within my technician position, guidance from my coworkers and friends, and repeatedly watching the *"no limits"* commercial on YouTube from Sun Microsystems is ultimately landed the three interviews that got me into the position.

When my girlfriend and I finally moved back into our home, we decided to marry. That was October of 2010. By May of 2011, we were divorced, she was pregnant with another man's child, and I had moved in with my close friend, Miser. *What happened?* Well, I didn't have my priorities straight. I was too focused on work. All of my hacking, exploits, and adventures were genuinely for the experience for my career. I mean sure, it was an addiction by now, but, what the hell? She said she was lying to me because she really didn't care anymore. All of the social networking and resume building, all were part of a bigger plan that I had brewing for the last decade. Now, all I had was nine boxes of stuff from my house, my bed, a tiny refrigerator that my step father had loaned me and was living in a house with cats that I was allergic to. Out of self-pity, I began drinking very heavily and smoking cigarettes again. I had lived in the same neighborhood as my house and I would periodically walk back to it, late at night, to just stare at it. I missed the dogs mostly.

I was now a "man without a country," as Ethermine put it. I had nothing left to strive for and fell into a deep depression. If it weren't for Miser, my brother and Ethermine, I probably wouldn't have made it through.

This is when I found out about LulzSec. They were a hacking group that hit the internet like a bat out of hell. Branched off from Anonymous, they had a classy in-your-face "fuck you" attitude. They wreaked havoc, mocked huge corporations and government organizations, and showed no fear. I too, I had nothing really to fear. I had nothing left for me. Why couldn't I participate in the new #AntiSec movement? I too have been raped by government funded organizations and police. I was sick of the amount of power they all sustained. I was starting to realize that the world I knew was falling apart. In the past few years, my online friend Fixer really opened my eyes to it all. I started noticing that I was being manipulated by corporations. News channels were spewing garbage and awful opinions trying to tell me how I feel about current affairs. Inflation and planned obsolescence had gotten the best of my income the last few years. I saw lying, manipulative leaders hoisting around nonsensical speeches and propaganda. Local government funded facilities raising costs and laying people off. *Fuck this.* Even if I could help in some small way, it may help take my mind off of my dull, pathetic life.

One night while drinking vodka and listening to music, I decided to look at the mass transit organization website for my city. This was a tax-dollar-funded organization that treated its patrons like shit, offered absolutely no security or safety measures, and was under constant change of wages. The media would blame the drivers who protested that it was the company responsible. The fee for taking mass transit was often increasing and the company cut back on the amount of available vehicles, forcing elderly and handicapped people to stand on the buses while the drivers flew like maniacs through the hills of the suburbs. *I found my target.*

Their website looked very old. It was themed in, what looked like, the nineteen nineties with poorly written HTML and CSS. After searching through the site for a few minutes I found a link with their search function that hit a database. It also used a simple GET request from the URL. I cracked a neighbor's WEP key to their FioS router and connected after spoofing my MAC address. Then, I let SQLMap fly on the URL. *That night I got it all. I got the code, files, database credentials, tables, columns, and everything in between.* I even had write access to the database, which meant I could easily deface the website with a kind #AntiSec message. But, I decided to wait. The fourth of July was coming up and that's when I decided that I would launch my attack.

As time went by, my friends and family did a great job at trying to cheer me up. I'll never forget that for the rest of my life. One night, my brother took me out and tried to get girls to like me. When I'd start talking to them, I just got easily annoyed and would say really random things. Eventually, I got severely drunk. That's not a good plan when trying to meet people, so I hear. Also, my phone had died and I was frequently trailing away from my group. At one point, I met a cute Italian girl who had a strange hairstyle. My brother and I talked with her as she walked back to her place and she said I could use her bathroom. While in her place, we talked a lot about the world, politics and freedom. She had a giant sized American flag on the wall in her room, which was otherwise bare, with a mattress on the floor. I don't know if it was the alcohol, the fact that I liked her views about everything, or that she was just cool in a dorky way, but I told her about the hack that I was going to do as part of the #AntiSec movement. I'm cringing now to think about it. This was a big mistake, albeit, she thought it was an awesome thing to do. We parted and, I'm not sure how but, I made it back to my friend's house.

The next day, I was schooled on the mistakes I made the night before and was told that I shouldn't get so drunk. When I recalled telling her about the hack, I shivered. I wanted to call it all off, just then.

Nights went by and, out of boredom, I started a brute force attack on an FTP server that was hosted by the mass transit web server. I let it go on from the neighbor's wireless access point *for days*. I'll never forget the one night, a few days into the brute force attack. I was relaxing on my roommate's porch in a deck chair smoking as five black cars with tiny police lights in the dashboards flew down the road heading straight for the neighbor's house that I was hacking from. All the same model car and all speeding about five feet away from each other in a row. *Holy Shit! Are those the party wagons!?* I ran back into the house, grabbed my netbook, antenna and external radio and flew out of the back door of his house. I ran up to the main road to catch a cab into the city and saw yet another one of the cars at the top of the street waiting. I ducked through backyards and made over to another way up to the main street. I connected to my screened IRSSI session with my phone and told my friends to remove all hacked data from the webserver. I then connected to my server and removed a huge amount of data out of shear paranoia.

As the cab came, thirty minutes later, I walked up to it and watched as the black car on the main street pull away. I told the driver he took too damn long and slammed the door without getting in. I had no reason to leave if the black cars were gone. Now, walking back towards my roommate's house, I threw my external USB adapter into a public garbage can after wiping it off completely with my jacket. I eventually made it safely back to his backyard and slipped back into his house through the back door in the basement. After which I connected to his wireless access point and went back to my IRC channel in my screened IRSSI session. Fixer told me that I was paranoid, but if they were really after me they would eventually find me.

With all of the hacked data gone and my nerves shot, I gave up on the hack. I decided to continue contributing to the movement and thought of another way I could help. Again, one night I was sitting on my roommate's porch and listening to a song called "Black Hole" from the Rosebuds with my headphones and drinking heavily. I was staring at the blinking lights of a local cell tower on the horizon and singing along. I was entranced by the scenery and music. The lyrics of the song gave me some clues about a legacy left behind of deception. *If all of the humans in the world disappeared all at once, wouldn't it be cool to have a ghost virus that continued to spread on its own?* Then, I thought about all of the millions of routers in the United States. *What if I could harness the fact that they mostly all overlap in many areas?* I thought about DD-WRT and my experience with the firmware. How it was installed, what it was capable of, and how it was open sourced, so I could completely customize my own version. *But wait. What about the firmware image I scored from the science lab down in the city?* Then, the Idea all came into place as the woman's voice on the mp3 in my phone sang gently into my ears through my headphones. I was going to, yet again, **raid the wireless empire**.

I darted back into his house and up to my room. I opened up one of the boxes that was still holding my belongings and pulled out my Verizon FioS router. This router is extremely abundant around me. It has the same exact admin password and an easy way to determine the WEP key right from the BSSID, or broadcasted MAC address in the beacon frames. *I was going to write a rapidly spreading wireless router virus.* Using the universal router image I stole from the scientific laboratory, I was going to install it, add software and recompile it.

After installing it onto a test router, I added code for the Aircrack-ng suite, scripts that brute forced the administrative passwords, and more. I was going to make it spread through very advanced http requests to the administrative firmware's web interface. As it spread, it would host a few files to automatically connect to my webserver online and begin the Python scripted flash process. I spent hours and hours coding, cracking and researching that night. I wrote code that would use Aircrack-ng and the Realtek-based radio to crack the WEP or WPA key by sending all handshakes to my online host. The host would attempt to crack the key, which is a beefy GPU powered Amazon EC2 server that used a 40GB wordlist, and return the key back to the router when completed. The router would be listening on a special high port: 31337 for the incoming key from the online server. Of course, this was only for a backup plan in case the router's password had been changed. The code also turned on port forwarding to all the open ports found on the LAN. All of this data, including the WAN IP, as the unique id, was dumped into a database on my online Linux VPS.

I coded it to not be too procedural. If the virus found a router that it couldn't hack into, it would simply stop and move onto the next one, by scanning the air for another victim. All of my scripts relied heavily on regular expressions and pure logic.

After a long night, the sun was about to come up and I started to feel the harsh effects of a hangover coming on. Pain set in behind my eyes and at the base of the back of my neck. Staying awake for extended amounts of time usually made me feel queasy. I decided I wasn't going to stop. I was fueled by my idea to get revenge on a world that had recently shat on me. So, I threw on my baseball hat and left the house to clear my mind. At a local convenience store I got some aspirin, a caffeinated drink, and some greasy food. Then, I made my way down to a baseball field and sat on the bleachers in the dark eating my food.

Now, I could feel my mind was completely blank. I felt numb again. I blamed the food and lit a cigarette. The sky started to turn pink and then orange before the sun finally crept over the hills towards my direction. I walked back to my roommate's house and looked at the router on the desk before falling on the bed into a deep sleep.

That morning I had a dream about how I could use engineering to prevent hackers from penetrating a wireless network. I could change the protocol to watch the power levels. If there was a certain discrepancy between the levels within a specific time threshold, then the packets would be dropped. This would prevent any external source from spoofing management frames and wreaking havoc in wireless LANs.

When I got up I dropped back down into my computer chair after drinking the rest of my soda. Yeah, I live in Pittsburgh and I say the word "soda." I started to reanalyze my code and make it smaller, tighter, and more efficient. I found some flaws that would make the virus not adaptable and fixed them along with adding more functionality. This was a huge project. Now, it was time to test it.

My grandparents were out of town and I knew they had a Verizon Fios Actiontec router I could use this for. After getting it and setting it up, I fired up my infected router. I started Airodump-ng on my Pirate Ship and watched as the infected router start to attack a completely different router! *Whoops!* I stopped it and modified the scripts to attack my grandparent's router specifically by BSSID. Then I started it back up again. Something wasn't right though. My online VPS wasn't responding correctly to the HTTP requests. I added some try-catch logic to the code and rewrote it through the now breaking day until I got it right. My grandparent's router finally came back up and dumped its credentials into my database!

I spent the rest of the twilight coding a login interface and PHP powered display page to watch the database change and fill up in real time. I added a few of my friends to the server and gave them all passwords so that they could watch it spread with me.

I re-flashed my grandparent's router with the backup image of it I had made and took it back over, while stopping for food at a pizza shop. When I finally got back to my roommate's house, I changed the code and database structure to store the following information:

Administration password	WAN IP	ESSID	BSSID	Machines on the LAN	opened ports

This way I could create stats, a bot to control them and more. I emailed my university and took two days off for the project. *This is going to be amazing. If this works, it will have changed lives, technology, and made an extreme effort in the revolution.*

That night I drank way too much. I can't even really recall all that happened. I woke up on bleachers at another baseball field completely drunk at around 4 am with no clue where I was or how I got there. The walk back to my roommate's house seemed to take forever. I landed on the deck chair on his front porch and studied the gold streetlights on the horizon waiting for them to converge into a single sober image. Before I knew it, I woke up on my bed in my room. I spent a while adjusting to everything and realized it was already about 2pm. I showered and made my way out to get food. As I returned, I was ready to start coding again. I finished the bot portion of the code, which I wrote in Perl and added functionality to DDoS any server I specified in an IRC channel. I made the bots all join the same channel and would issue commands as ! command. Since I didn't include this bot code into the router firmware image, I would host it on the same compromised webserver that had the PHP scripts and just issue a simple wget to retrieve it. I then tested the MySQL database that was to host all of my victim's information. I thought about how this virus could potentially spread all the way across the north eastern United States. *How would I tell besides using this page? Should I change the ESSIDs? No then, someone would suspect it and possibly take down the router.* I will stick with the PHP site. I was polishing it up and making adjustments when I realized that I could go no further. I needed more food. I was just coding for the last 7 hours straight on just Diet Coke.

I entered a convenience store and saw a friend behind the counter. I asked her if she wanted to hang out after she got off work and she agreed. That night we sat together in a cemetery-church parking lot smoking and talking about comedians and music together. Then something unusual happened. As we talked we heard the clicking of animal hooves out in the concrete parking lot. As we looked we saw an adult female deer! Pittsburgh had a lot of areas that were still covered in trees and some dense wooded areas, so it wasn't that odd to see a deer roaming around in the city. But, it surprised the hell out of us and we stared in awe. The timing was awesome and truly what I needed.

The next day was the big day. I woke up sober and early. I started writing a document about the new wireless security method I dreamt about two nights before. When I was done, I entered IRC channels and forums to tell my friends what I was planning to do. None of them believed me and as we chatted and laughed, I was now drinking heavily. No matter how drunk I was in the early part of this day, my mind was crystal clear and my thoughts were like spears against the unknown. I thought about my impromptu date last night and decided to name my creation the WiFirus. As the evening fell and the sun draped shadows and bright gold light across the hills in which I lived, I pressed the red button on my Flipcam and began a self-documentation of this hack. It was attached to a tripod on the end of the porch and I sat in a large white Adirondack chair, with a tall glass of vodka and cranberry juice. There was a non-infected Actiontec router sitting right next to me, my laptop on the white table with the booze and juice, and my netbook was on the porch floor next to me.

Video Foot☠ge

The following section was taken from a digital recording device.

I sat there without words gazing out at the cell tower on the horizon and it's forever blinking lights. Finally I said, "Hello, it's July something, 2011. I am Seadog and this is my story." I took a huge gulp from the glass finishing it off and put it down onto a white table. I then stood up and showed the camera my large 14dbi panel antenna that was attached to a tall tripod. "This antenna stretches rather far in most normal conditions. In this region, which is littered with large hills, it should reach to each visible house on each side of this valley."

I showed the computer screen that was a blinking terminal that had `./wifirus` waiting to be executed. All I had to do was hit return on the keyboard. "Am I just another lost cause?" "Has this country killed all of those who truly believes that we can think freely?" I began pouring vodka into the glass, but left the cranberry juice alone. I staggered and showed the hills. "I am sorry, but I have to borrow… ..your .. network. Wireless. The. Wireless networks for a few days, mmkay?" I stammered and then laughed. I drank almost half of my glass before letting out a pirate-like "yarr!!!" and hit enter on my keyboard. I noticed the LEDs on the router I had plugged into the wall turn from green to red to green again and snickered. I sat on the chair with my netbook and opened Google Chrome to access the PHP page on the compromised site. Before logging in, I opened a new terminal and started Airodump-ng on the channel of the router. The router was injecting packets to another nearby router already. I logged into the site and saw only the router sitting next to me listed. The very first wireless router to be infected with WiFirus was by my side. Then just a second later I jumped up out of my chair and poured another glass of straight vodka and lit a cigarette. I casually walked over to the camera and said calmly, "It has begun. The virus has already spread to another router" and smiled widely with my eye lids half closed.

I drank heavily and began singing pirate-themed songs and talking in a pirate voice. I look at the screen and said "five more victims!" Then, I put the cigarette down and sat in the chair. I told my friends on IRC that I did it that it was working. I gave them the key to the channel #wifirus and they joined to see each bot connected with their respective ESSID as their nicknames. If there was a duplicate the IRC server appended an underscore. I typed !curl http://somelongdeadvictimwebsite.com/hidden/couter.php and then accessed the page with my own browser. Its count was up to 8, which was how many bots were in the channel. The routers were now under my command! This would increase the "counter number" I added to the page that everyone was logged into. An AJAX script would periodically update the values on the screen showing more and more machines connecting. If I, or anyone else, hit the counter button, it would test the bots by forcing them all to hit the PHP counter page to prove they were all mine.

At this point, I was completely drunk. My friends were all laughing on IRC about it all and I felt what, I could only describe, as if I were glowing. I had goose-bumps and couldn't stop smiling. I felt the numbness and tingling rush over the top of my head and around passed my ears. *I did it. I fucking did it.* Then I began to sing again. This time it was loud and distorted the sound in the Flipcam. Singing like a pirate I started dancing with my legs and arms. This carried on for about an hour or so. I would dance, laugh, sing and scream out of the deck and then take a break while drinking and smoking.

After displaying myself like a fool, I tripped over the cable to the netbook and it fell to the porch floor. I too stumbled over it and my foot landed right onto the screen which was bent backwards. Someone from across the street laughed loudly and I turned my head towards him. There were many people on their front deck and several other porches watching me and the whole time I didn't notice – until now.

"What?! Huh?! What the fuck are you all staring at?! I wouldn't be so depressed if my life were as shitty and mundane as yours!" I yelled. I stumbled up and started grabbing my equipment from the floor and table. Someone yelled something that I didn't even hear but I still took offense to it, yelling back "Mind your own fucking business you unimaginative, corporate owned, meatbag," I said loudly, but not yelling. "I am enjoying my victory against those who oppress you! Yeah that's right. I am fighting for my freedom. What the fuck are you doing with your time, collecting welfare?" I said in almost tears.

I was in a dark place. A very, very dark place. I realized that I was in a roommate's house, who took me in when I needed help and now I bet am making his neighbors hate him. I am screwing up everywhere I look and turn. I didn't even know what day it was.

Fa☠lling In ___

I made my way up the stairs and threw the equipment onto the pile of boxes on the floor. The nine boxes that held every physical thing I had to show for my life. I pulled the corked cap out of the vodka bottle and drank right from its lips. Then I dropped the bottle and staggered over to the bed turning around. I put my arms out to my sides and fell backwards onto the bed falling through it.

I fell straight through the mattress.

I looked up and saw the room getting smaller and smaller as I free fell into total blackness. I watched the remaining light from the room above as it lit the sides of the comforter that was flapping away on either side of me in the wind from the fall. The flapping blanket sound was somewhat soothing. I felt my hair was blowing around and felt strangely calm and relaxed. *I don't care what happens.* I fell for about a minute and a half before I just closed my eyes in utter defeat. Just then, the wind stopped and the flapping noise of the comforter changed into the creaking of old wood. It sounded like an old wood floor of a house that was straining each time the wind blew. I smelled wet wood and ropes. The scent reminded me of when I was a child in the summertime, waiting in the long lines for the watery wooden ride called the Log Jammer at Kennywood Park. I opened my eyes and realized I was on a large, antique wooden pirate ship. Instantly, I was in complete awe by the sight of it all. There were chests, wound up ropes, masts, sails, railings and cannons. *How the hell did I get here? Am I dead?* "Doug." a soft female voice said. I turned and saw my friend that I had the casual date with, the night before. "Hey." "This boat is awesome," I said. She was sitting on a pile of wound rope around an old-fashioned wooden barrel in a long dress that hung over it all. She was holding a large strange stringed instrument from which she began to play the Rosebuds song that inspired my hack, "Black Hole."

I felt a tear hit my cheek and just stood there as she played. I turned and walked, over a large Sun Microsystems logo on the floorboards, to the edge of the ship and leaned against the railing, staring down below. The ship was in the air, bound to a small planet's orbit who's diameter couldn't have been longer than five or six lengths of the ship itself. The land below was so beautiful. There were strands of green and blue Christmas lights in every tree. The colors of the grass, roads, walkways and humble houses were all muted but vivid with patterns. Every now and then I would feel a soothing breeze of air hit me and it smelled like a cotton shirt full of static electricity. "Where are we, exactly?" I asked. "The Other Side," she responded and began to sing just like the woman from the song she was playing. There were small whales "swimming" in the air around the planet and I saw the feint glow every now and then from, what I thought were, fireflies close to the planets trees and grass. Light from a nearby star sprinkled twilight on the small planet, blinking the edges of small ponds and shooting gold strands through branches of trees.

People, dogs, and small rabbits moved about in what seemed like the most perfect "daily lives" I could ever imagine. As the ship slowly moved over the planet, I saw a small cemetery and large weeping willow trees. The sight made me feel jealous, honestly. *I wanted that life.* I wanted to be there. "Wow," I stammered. We could see so many stars around us, and a small moon that was tethered to the planet via a slow orbit. I saw a picnic and as we moved closer I realized it was my family on the blanket eating and talking. They were there without me.

After a few minutes, I walked back as the song was ending and sat next to her. She placed the instrument on the pile next to her and looked straight ahead. "I know," I sighed. "I know why I am here, and I want to stay here," I said. Just then, I felt my phone vibrating in my pocket but ignored it. She pointed to, what looked like, a bright star in the sky and said "Stop that." I stared at it and realized that it was a, slowly growing, small tear in the black blanket of the universe. "What? What is that," I said as I stood up looking in its direction.

All at once, I was knocked down and a loud siren sound pierced my ears as the tear in the blanket above ripped the entire scene directly in half.

No! No! No! No!

The real universe was thrusting its weight upon me again, as if on cue *Why the hell should I have any fun, right?* As the light above became brighter and brighter, I put my arm over to cover my eyes and slowly the world I was in started to morph into my room at my roommate's house. The alarm was going off as I struggled to get out of bed. I turned and hit the button and sat back down catching my face in the palms of my hands as my knees held my elbows up. I thought about the dream for a few minutes and then plugged my phone into the wall, turning it on. I could barely stand up straight and felt extremely light headed.

When I saw the date, I realized that I had just slept for 15 straight hours. *Jesus, what the hell happened? Why the fuck was my alarm even set?* I went into the bathroom and stood in the front of the sink washing my face and just looking back at my reflection in the mirror above it. I walked back to the room and sat back on the bed pulling open my laptop and logging into the PHP interface for my botnet. The counter was now in the thousands. I switched over to the IRC channel and saw my friends were trying to wake me up. They were eagerly begging me to test its power. When they saw I wasn't responding they joked that I was v&. I typed !ddos usa.gov and hit enter. Immediately an4lyS1S said ":D yes! You're back!" I opened a browser and saw that I couldn't access the site and asked if he could. "hahahah it's outty!" He replied. It was incapacitated from the massive amount of requests from all of the hacked routers across the north eastern US. To my surprise, the PHP interface indicated that the virus was actually still spreading!

So...

*...how far will **this** go?*

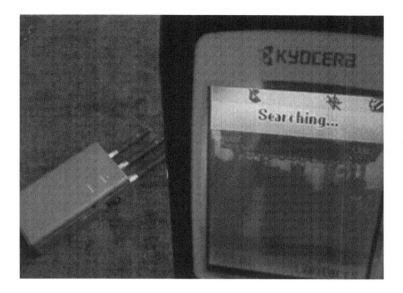

Figure 0. One of the cellphone signal jammers in action. Chapter 7

Figure 1. The WiFirus Routers. Chapter 12

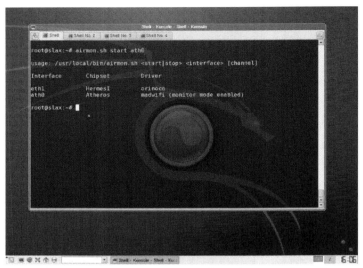

Figure 2. The Christophe Devine video of cracking WEP key. Chapter 1

Figure 3. The Pirate Ship. Photo taken in the mall where Seadog worked. – Chapters 1,7

Figure 4. "snowpocalypse" the 10th st. bridge leading into the Armstrong tunnels which was usually very heavily used. Chapter 11.

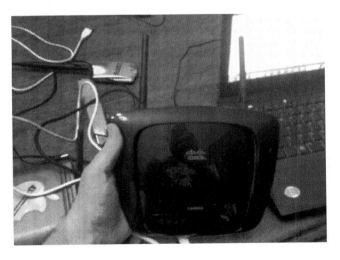

Figure 5. Router used in Chapter 11 – Cisco 160NL

Figure 6. From top right to left then down, Seadog phreaking, the early phone phreaking website from chapter 1,the "don't forget to spoof your MAC address" sticker, Seadog in a "can" and climbing a telephone pole to get into TNIs, Ethermine opening the can for Seadog, beigeboxing from a payphone, a 2600Hz box for seizing a trunk from an old switch, and finally redboxing form a payphone.

Gloss☠ry of Terms

- ☠ **#Antisec** - a movement opposed to the computer security industry.
- ☠ **31337 / 1337 / L33t / r33t** – different forms of the word "elite" written in the "leet" language.
- ☠ **4chan** – best imageboard ever.
- ☠ **802.11** - set of standards for implementing wireless local area network (WLAN) computer communication in the 2.4, 3.6 and 5 GHz frequency bands
- ☠ **ALFA** - Alfa was established in 2002 and remains a highly motivated company dedicated to the innovative design and manufacturing of high performance yet cost-effective Local/Wide Area (LAN/WAN) products.
- ☠ **AP** – Wireless Access Point
- ☠ **ARP** – Address Resolution Protocol – used for address related tasks in a TCP/IP network
- ☠ **AWK, SED, GREP** – text manipulation programs that are standard among Linux and UNIX like operating system and their shells.
- ☠ **Aircrack-ng Suite** - network software suite consisting of a detector, packet sniffer, WEP and WPA/WPA2-PSK cracker and analysis tool for 802.11 wireless LANs
- ☠ **Auditor** – Deprecated version of Linux used for security and penetration testing.
- ☠ **BSSID** – Basic Service Set Identifier – MAC address of the Access Point.
- ☠ **Backtrack** - a distribution based on the Debian GNU/Linux distribution aimed at digital forensics and penetration testing use
- ☠ **Bash** - a Unix shell written by Brian Fox for the GNU Project as a free software replacement for the Bourne shell (sh).
- ☠ **Beige Box** - a device that is technically equivalent to a telephone company lineman's handset — a telephone fitted with alligator clips to attach it to a line.
- ☠ **Bot / Botnet** - software applications that run automated tasks over the Internet.
- ☠ **CTRL+D / CTRL+C / CTRL+Z** – Control characters for logging out, stopping an application, and sending an application to the background in a standard Linux shell – respectively.
- ☠ **CUDA** - a parallel computing platform and programming model created by NVIDIA.

- ☠ **Cellphone Jammer** – a device that intentionally emits radio frequency signals to interfere with the operation of other radio communications by saturating its receiver with noise or false information
- ☠ **CyanogenMod** - open source replacement firmware for smart phones and tablet computers based on the Androidmobile operating system.
- ☠ **DOS** - disk operating system (generically), most often abbreviated as DOS, refer to an operating system software used in most computers that provides the abstraction and management of secondary storage devices and the information on them (e.g., file systems for organizing files of all sorts)
- ☠ **Debian** - computer operating system composed of software packages released as free and open source software primarily under theGNU General Public License along with other free software licenses.
- ☠ **DoS / DDoS** - denial-of-service attack (DoS attack) or distributed denial-of-service attack (DDoS attack) is an attempt to make a machine or network resource unavailable to its intended users
- ☠ **Dsniff** - set of password sniffing and network traffic analysis tools written by security researcher and startup founder Dug Song to parse different application protocols and extract relevant information
- ☠ **EC2** - Elastic Compute Cloud (EC2) is a central part of Amazon.com's cloud computing platform, Amazon Web Services (AWS)
- ☠ **ESSID** – Extended Service Set identifier – name of wireless network. E.g. "Linksys" or "NETGEAR"
- ☠ **Ettercap-ng** - free and open source network security tool for man-in-the-middle attacks on LAN
- ☠ **Figlet** - a computer program that generates text banners, in a variety of typefaces, composed of letters made up of conglomerations of smaller ASCII characters (see ASCII art)
- ☠ **Fragrouter**
- ☠ **GPU** - graphics processing unit (GPU), also occasionally called visual processing unit (VPU), is a specialized electronic circuit designed to rapidly manipulate and alter memory to accelerate the building of images in a frame buffer intended for output to a display.
- ☠ **Google Dork** – Special string of characters used in advanced Google Searches that can reveal a massive amount of information not normally viewable by a simple search.
- ☠ **IP** - Internet Protocol (IP) is the principal communications protocol used for relaying datagrams (also known as network packets) across an internetwork using the Internet Protocol Suite responsible for routing

packets across network boundaries.

- ☠ **IRC** - Internet Relay Chat (IRC) is a protocol for real-time Internet text messaging (chat) or synchronous conferencing.
- ☠ **IRSSI** - an IRC client program for Linux, FreeBSD, Microsoft Windows, and Mac OS X.
- ☠ **ISP** – Internet Service Provider – e.g. VeriZon, or Comcast
- ☠ **LCD** – Liquid Crystal Display
- ☠ **LED** – Light Emitting Diode
- ☠ **LMMFAO** – "Laughing my mother fucking ass off"
- ☠ **Linux** – a Unix-like computer operating system assembled under the model of free and open source software development and distribution
- ☠ **LulzSec** - is a computer hacker group that claimed responsibility for several high profile attacks, including the compromise of user accounts from Sony Pictures in 2011.
- ☠ **Metasploit Framework / Meterpreter / Msfconsole** - a computer security project which provides information about security vulnerabilities and aids in penetration testing and IDS signaturedevelopment.
- ☠ **Mudkip** - a Pokémon species in Nintendo and Game Freak's Pokémon franchise.
- ☠ **Multimeter** - also known as a VOM (Volt-Ohm meter), is an electronic measuring instrument that combines several measurement functions in one unit.
- ☠ **NMAP** - a security scanner originally written by Gordon Lyon (also known by his pseudonym Fyodor Vaskovich)[1] used to discover hostsand services on a computer network, thus creating a "map" of the network
- ☠ **Netcat** - a computer networking service for reading from and writing network connections using TCP or UDP. Netcat is designed to be a dependable "back-end" device that can be used directly or easily driven by other programs and scripts.
- ☠ **Netsh** - a command-line utility included in Microsoft's Windows NT line of operating systems beginning with Windows 2000.
- ☠ **OMFG** – "Oh my fuckin' god"
- ☠ **OS** – Operating System – e.g. Microsoft Windows, Mac OSX, GNU Linux, and Oracle/Sun Solaris
- ☠ **OpenWRT** - an operating system primarily used on embedded devices to route network traffic.
- ☠ **PBX** – Private Branch Exchange - a telephone exchange that serves a particular business or office, as opposed to one that a common carrier or telephone company operates for many businesses or for the general

public.
- ☠ **PC** – Personal Computer
- ☠ **PCMCIA** - Personal Computer Memory Card International Association, the PC Card standard as well as its successors were defined and developed by the Personal Computer Memory Card International Association (PCMCIA), which itself was created by a number of computer industry companies in 1986 by Jacob D. Holm
- ☠ **Phone Losers of America** - an American phreaking group founded in the 1990s, active on the hacking scene.
- ☠ **Phone Phreaking**
- ☠ **Pyrit** - allows to create massive databases, pre-computing part of the IEEE 802.11 WPA/WPA2-PSK authentication phase in a space-time-tradeoff. Exploiting the computational power of Many-Core- and other platforms through ATI-Stream, Nvidia CUDA and OpenCL, it is currently by far the most powerful attack against one of the world's most used security-protocols.
- ☠ **RF** – Radio Frequency
- ☠ **RFi / LFi** – Remote and Local File inclusion attack. This is when an HTTP request method parameter is altered in forcing the webserver to display files on the webservers operating system, or run files stored remotely as if they were intended to locally by the web application.
- ☠ **Rake / pick / tension wrench** – Lock picking tools
- ☠ **Ralink / Atheros / Realtek / Broadcom Chip Sets** – type of radio chip in a wireless device. It designed to work with a specific family of microprocessors, Because it controls communications between the processor and external devices, the chipset plays a crucial role in determining system performance
- ☠ **RoadKil** – RoadKil.net
- ☠ **SMB** – Server Message Block operates as an application-layer network protocol[1] mainly used for providing shared access to files, printers, serial ports, and miscellaneous communications between nodes on a network. It also provides an authenticated inter-process communication mechanism
- ☠ **SMBTREE** – tool used to discover Windows and Linux shares that use the SMB protocol.
- ☠ **SQL** – Structured Query Language – commonl language used among databases used for Web Applications and sites.
- ☠ **SQLMap** - an open source penetration testing tool that automates the process of detecting and exploiting SQL injection flaws and taking over of database servers.

- **SQLi** – SQL Injection
- **SSID** – Service Set Identifier – broadcasted name of wireless network – used interchangeably with ESSID
- **SSLStrip** – Advanced Man In the Middle Attack that prevents a browser from upgrading to an SSL connection in a subtle way that would likely go unnoticed by a user.
- **Skiddy / Script Kiddy** - individuals who use scripts or programs developed by others to attack computer systems and networks and deface websites.
- **Social Engineering** - the art of manipulating people into performing actions or divulging confidential information.
- **THC Hydra** - very fast network logon cracker which support many different services.
- **TNI** – Telephone Network Interface – commonly found outdoors within the close vicinity of the subscriber or a large box full of many subscriber terminals.
- **Tarball** - a file format (in the form of a type of archive bitstream) and the name of a program used to handle such files
- **Trojan / Backdoor** - a malicious application that masquerades as a legitimate file or helpful program but whose real purpose is, for example, to grant a attacker (computer security)|hacker]] unauthorized access to a computer
- **VDC** – Volts in DC
- **Vim** – vi editor improved
- **WAN** – Wide Area network or group of LANs
- **WEP / WPA / WPA2 / CCMP** - security protocols and security certification programs developed by the Wi-Fi Alliance to secure wireless computer networks.
- **WHAX!** – deprecated distribution of Linux used for security and penetration testing.
- **Wardriving** - the act of searching for Wi-Fi wireless networks by a person in a moving vehicle, using a portable computer, smartphone or personal digital assistant (PDA).
- **WiFi** - a popular technology that allows an electronic device to exchange data wirelessly (using radio waves) over acomputer network, including high-speed Internet connections.
- **Wireshark** - a free and open-source packet analyzer. It is used for network troubleshooting, analysis, software and communications protocoldevelopment, and education. Originally named Ethereal, in May 2006 the project was renamed Wireshark due to trademark issues.

- ☠ **XSS** – Cross Site Scripting attack, which can make an attacker inject code into a database, deface a website using special HTTP parameters, or force an unsuspecting users browser to execute Javascript code.
- ☠ **Suicide / black / grey / white hats** - Several subgroups of the computer underground with different attitudes use different terms to demarcate themselves from each other, or try to exclude some specific group with which they do not agree.

Ac☠nowledgments

Douglas Berdeaux would like to thank the following, in no specific order.

Julie Aluise, Fixer, Thomas Berdeaux, Victoria and David Weis, Douglas Berdeaux, Jaime and Lynn McLain, Paul (Miser) Werkmeister, Ethermine, Joe Satovich, Joe Ball, Arkasia Yoann, Ronin Harris, Michael Gigantor, Vladimir Mollov, Grant Stone, Jake Tullis, Don Maue, Brad Carter, Murd0c, iBall, RTF, chartreuse, g0d0t, altalp, androsyn, elsif, noghri, genetic, Beth Ussery, Sarah Hodge, tekk, mad, BJ, An4lYS1S, mixi, mad, rogueclown, John Allen Paulos, Adam Sluk, #2600, #lunatics, and Grrly. I dedicate this work to all of you.

20733218R00068

Made in the USA
Lexington, KY
16 February 2013